Eric Devine

This Side of Normal

Long Tale Press, LLC
Redmond, Washington

Text set in Adobe Garamond Pro
Designed by Nathan Everett

10 9 8 7 6 5 4 3 2

For my wife, Carrie. For never losing faith. For allowing me to dream. For knowing that our children would alter our life in a wonderful way. You have given me all that I need.

For my parents. This is, in part, our story. Thank you for showing me how to live.

For every "Ed," his family, his friends: Each day is unique, in the myriad ways this disease presents itself. Embrace that element, and one another.

Part One: Acute

Chapter 1

If you can look into the seeds of time
And say which grain will grow and which will not,
Speak, then, to me, who neither beg nor fear
Your favors nor your hate. (Macbeth, 1.3.61-64)

IT'S THE MIDDLE OF THE NIGHT, and I'm in bed trying not to piss myself. I'm like my grandfather. Just the other day he told my mom that he's up "draining the lizard" every few hours. "It's like a hose that's stuck on trickle. No matter what I do I can't shut it off. That can't be normal." He cleared his throat to close his point. I nodded. Not at the phlegm. He's always doing that. At what he meant. Not having the plumbing working correctly. That's my problem. I'm up three to six times a night. And it's not a nervous, little, annoying pee.

Lately, it's as if I'm in a marathon-pissing contest. Except I'm the only contestant. It wouldn't be so bad if I had a bank of snow in my bathroom. That way I could write my name with my piss. But no, it's just me, the cold linoleum floor, the creak of the house, and the sound of a flood pouring into the toilet.

I'm staring at my walls to distract myself. They're covered in this god-awful underwater/ocean wallpaper. I never should have listened to my mom. "It'll look so cool! We can use the fishing gear from Uncle Brian as the focus to the theme." She's way into Martha Stewart. Sad. I know. But she's got to have something to do besides working all the goddamn time. She's a nurse. Judging from what the job has done to her, I know that's one career path I won't be taking.

Her pain is all in the eyes. They get so clouded over that she looks vacant. Her thoughts retreat from them. She watches home improvement shows and reads her home decorating magazines. Often she'll dive into little projects to keep her hands busy while her mind filters out her day. Then there's my dad. He watches sports obsessively. Non-stop. Enough said. The two of them. Her with the projects. Him with the sports. They never meet.

But it's more than just different interests. They can't seem to put their relationship back together. Not since my Uncle Brian died. His death has changed everything. How my parents get along. How my dad feels about me. I'd like to change that. Help them get fixed. Help my dad to see what's in front of him. Not just the past. But I can't get into that now. My bladder feels as if it's weighted down by a bowling ball and filled with cracked glass.

I peel back the covers and slide my legs over the edge of the bed. My feet hit the carpet and it's like I'm three years old again. Afraid I'm going to have an "accident." Except, at fifteen I don't think you can call it that anymore. I bolt from bed. That was a bad move. It's like a sword has been jammed into my midsection. My legs buckle. Fortunately, the bathroom isn't very far. I plod down the hall and shuffle in. I rip off my shorts and don't bother to shut the door or hit the light.

I land on the toilet with a thud. The tank's lid smacks the wall. I don't care. I've made it, and now… *Oh Holy God! Yes!* I rest my face against the cool top of the tank. I'm on the toilet backwards.

I've been up like this for a month now. At first it was no big deal. Soon, though, I got tired from all the pushing. I sat. Now, I'm exhausted. Therefore, I just plop down and rest my arms or head on the tank. I then let gravity work down below. This way, at least for a few moments, I'm free. The pressure spills out until it's gone. I snooze through it.

Then I flush it all away.

I find my shorts with my toes. Slip them on. Run my hands quickly under the faucet. There's no time to think. Just rush. I want to get back to bed and fall asleep. Because maybe. Just maybe. I'll sleep so soundly that I won't wake up again. I won't have to see three, four, five, and six o'clock. Hell, I'd settle for waking up to a wet bed if it meant I wouldn't have to be so damn tired.

I slap the faucet off and take a step toward the door. There's a creak from my parents' bed across the hall. The light pops on. I freeze like a deer. I do a quick inventory of my shorts, making sure that they're actually there. I've forgotten before. My mom appears. She's like Medusa. I look at her shoulders, her hands, her feet, but never directly into her face when she's fresh from bed. I did, once. I swear I was marbled for a good five minutes. Her hair is a tangled mass that is trying to run away from the scalp. Bassett hounds have nothing on her when it comes to droopy, puffy eyelids. Despite all this, she wants to talk. "Ed, what are you doing up?"

Why this question? I'm coming from the bathroom. Isn't it obvious? "I had to go." I register her shoulder. It's still. I make a move to pass. "G'night!"

"How many times is that?"

I stop cold. That's the thing about parents. Or maybe it's just my mom. She always has a sense about what I'm up to. Even when I was hiding out in the basement. As quiet as a mute. Looking at those dirty magazines—which I still swear were Sid's—she saw the guilt written all over my face. Or maybe just in the eyes. I half turn to her. "Three."

She sighs. Her toes wriggle up off the floor. "Okay, go to bed."

I lie on my back. My side. Practically on my head. All in an effort to get comfortable. It's useless. I can already feel the pressure mounting. Now I'm worried that the next time I go to the bathroom she'll be listening. Only this time, she'll tell me the complete opposite of what she told my grandfather. "You're fine. It's completely normal for someone your age to be up like that."

I stare out the window into the swirling night. My throat fills. I try to clear it.

I was up three more times during the night. I passed by my parents' bedroom and pretended I didn't hear sighs coming from within. Now I'm back in the bathroom. *Where else would I be?* My reflection is dreadful. I've got the worn out look of the overachievers at school. The ashen grey circles that cup my eyes look the same as their all-nighter appearance. I turn away and take in "the head" as my Gramps calls it. I truly wish we had a nicer one. My friend Sid has a gigantic bathroom, with a whirlpool tub and marble tile on the floor and walls. It's a friggin' quarry in there. The last time I stayed over at Sid's I stood on the tile and felt the cold through my feet. His house is pin-drop quiet. The bathroom has like five windows. The moonlight was pouring in. I looked around and thought...*It's so beautiful.* I didn't want to leave. But I was just beginning my nightly courtship with the toilet. Sid's, by far, blows mine out of the water.

My bathroom's a complete disaster. Toothbrushes and combs lie next to one another on the white-speckled counter, alternately swapping paste and hair. I've brushed my teeth with errant strands of my mom's Medusa locks on countless occasions. My dad's electric razor is permanently plugged into the one outlet in the entire room. It dangles alongside the vanity, spewing bits of facial hair like pepper across the floor. The mirror is never clean. It's always coated with that same, elusive, white speckle. It's like looking at my reflection through snowflakes.

After my first time at Sid's, back when I was a kid, I asked my mom why our house was such a mess. She stared at me in the rearview mirror. Her glare iced the windows. "Sid's parents are very fortunate." That's it. That's all she said. I sat there wondering what the hell she meant. Were they fortunate because they had a lot of money? Or because they have a nice house? Or because they had Sid and not me? If she only knew what it's really like over there.

Anyway, here I am in the wadded-up-Kleenex-that-should-be-thrown-out bathroom, staring at my face. I've seen pictures of the Holocaust. I'd totally blend in. All I'd need is one of those pajama outfits and a yellow star. I'm gaunt like that. But I haven't always been this way. I mean, I've never been overweight, except for when I was a baby. Even then it was normal fat, not on-the-cover-of-the-*National-Enquirer*-with-Bat-boy-fat. Now I'm rail-thin. My eyes and cheeks are sunken into my face. I look like some model trying for a sexy pose. Except on me, it's gross. Not at all sexy.

I step out into the hall. *Sportscenter* blares from the kitchen.

"Jesus!" my dad yells at the T.V.

"No, it's just me." It's a little joke. My dad misses it and strains further to watch the play in slow-motion. I walk over to the counter where my mom is cursing at the black, crusty mess on her plate. I pull from the cabinet a box of some generic frosted concoction and set it down next to my mom's plate. She gives me a quick, "Hmmph," and proceeds to throw away her burned breakfast. She leaves the room without having eaten.

I grab a bowl, a spoon, the milk from the fridge, and bring it all to the table. I sit down next to my father. It's like being next to a corpse. He's so thoroughly cold. I slurp away at my cereal. He mutters over his coffee mug at the commentators on the screen. "You…uh…catch anything, fishing?" He went over the weekend. It's worth a shot. The cereal puckers my cheeks and hurts my jaw. I wait for his answer. He shifts in his seat and speaks without looking at me.

"No… I…" but he doesn't finish. His jaw works for a second. The muscle twitches. He turns to me and his eyes are flints. I clutch my spoon. He gets up, scraping the chair legs across the floor, and is gone.

Stupid ass. I'm not sure if it's directed at him or me. The fishing gear in my room was so I could join him and his brother, my Uncle Brian, on these weekend fishing trips. That obviously isn't going to happen. For more reasons than just that my gear is on the wall. It's after 7:00. Time to go to school.

I piss again before I grab my backpack and leave. It's a cool morning. The beginning of November. My breath hangs in transparent clouds as I walk. The dew on the grass is clumped. Congealed. Close to freezing.

Sid's already at the bus stop when I roll up. I fall into a heap next

5

to him. "Hey." He juts his chin. I reply with the same, sniffle, and wait for more. I never know with Sid. His parents argue a lot and he typically reflects the state of things at home. His parents are that classic stereotype. Rich and unhappy. What does that make my parents? We're broke, and I don't think they say more than ten words at a time to each other.

Sid's like a stone today. His back is to me, picking up the morning sun. He stares down the street, looking as if he's watching for the approaching bus.

I sniffle again and pull into myself. The pressure is mounting down below. My mouth is chalky. My stomach growls. Sid and I sit in the cold November morning and say nothing.

I'm in tenth grade, so it suffices to say I hate school. Every day, it's the same damn drama. It wasn't always this way. It started to get weird in eighth grade, when the girls began to sprout boobs. I say, "sprout" because that's what it was like. One day, hey, we're playing wiffle ball, yelling at the girls to get out of the outfield. The next, it's, "Hey! Did you see the rack on Stacy?" Of course this has been followed with all the attempts at hooking up. Or unsuccessfully trying to hook up. Which only leads to more drama.

Sid and I swim with the tide of students out of homeroom. Wash into the hall. Drift into Science. We usually sit in the back. But lately he's been trying to hook up with the aforementioned Stacy. He sits near her and her empty-headed friends, Ashley and Brittany. I can't stand any of them, especially Stacy—no self-respect. Sid doesn't care.

I've been sitting next to this kid Mark. He's always drawing in this sketchbook of his. Never paying attention in class. Or so it seems. Whenever no one feels like answering a question—usually some big, who-the-hell-knows kind of a question, one that could clog a toilet or put a know-it-all grin on just about any teacher—he nails the answer. Just snaps his head up. Brushes his bangs aside. Says it. Answers like he's always known. Then, just as quickly, he returns to his doodling.

I move to the back and sit. Mark looks up. "Hey." He returns to his drawing. My teacher, Mrs. Didi, asks Sid something. Before he can answer, the tools come in. Ashley, Brittany, and Stacy flounce past Mrs. Didi, laughing their stupid, attention-grabbing laughs. They're barely dressed. Stomachs exposed with belly shirts. Low cut jeans that are a sneeze away from falling off. I'd like the appearance more if their superiority wasn't glistening all over it.

Sid's grinning like Tony the Tiger. Mrs. Didi's got that sad/frustrated/almost-angry look. Teachers have a patent on it. Maybe it's a genetic thing. The way their mouths can smile but the rest of their face can tell an entirely different story. Sid follows them without answering Mrs. Didi. She shakes her head. Her nostrils flare. She's inhaled the uninviting aroma of stale cigarettes masked in perfume that trails from the trio.

The bell rings and Mrs. Didi stands before the board, where she's written *CELL RESPIRATION*. I have no idea what the hell cell respiration is. I really don't care. I have to piss. But the slackers shuffle in. Mrs. Didi frowns. I lose the energy to raise my hand.

"Take out your notebooks class. There will be a quiz after."

We always have quizzes. Right after we write down the notes she puts on the board. About what we've just written down. She actually expects us to learn this way. I don't even bother to moan like half the class does.

Mrs. Didi blabs on and on about Cell Respiration. This cartoon image pops into my head: all these little cells. Swimming around in my body. Inhaling and exhaling at the same time. Like some micro-level yoga class. I chuckle.

Mark's head snaps up. He's like a prairie dog checking for danger. He twists to me. His eyes are slits.

"What?" I shrug.

He leans closer. "What you laughing at?" His arm is curled around his sketchbook. The curve of a woman's hip peeks from the crook of his elbow.

"Nothing. Just a stupid picture-thing I was making up about this respiration crap."

Mrs. Didi pauses and looks at me. She may call on me. My stomach flops. That's not good. I still have to piss. But she's just waiting for the class to catch up. Sid's bent over his desk, whispering something to Stacy. The others look as blank as the pages of their notebooks. Mrs. Didi resumes whatever the hell she was going on about. I look at my own notebook. I haven't even opened it.

"What do you mean?" Mark's voice is a gravelly whisper.

I turn to him. "Huh?"

He leans in. "The picture. What'd you see?"

I can't believe I'm having this conversation. "A bunch of cells... breathing in and out." I pause and nod toward the board. "You know, cell respiration. It's stupid."

Mark doesn't say anything, just looks off into space. I wait. He shoots me another look. Grins. Flips over a new page in his sketchbook. In an instant he's back into his comfort zone. I get around to lifting up my arm to go to the bathroom. Mrs. Didi begins to pass out our quizzes. No point asking now. I lower my arm. I write my name on the paper I'm handed. Before I can answer the first question Mark slams his finished quiz on the corner of his desk. He returns to his drawing. I shake my head and read questions about mitosis and meiosis.

I have absolutely no idea. They sound like diseases that old people get. That pharmaceutical companies then create drugs for. That ad agencies then create commercials for, with purple-haired grannies and saggy-assed gramps walking down the beach holding hands. Luckily the quiz is multiple-choice. I pick mostly "C."

"Hey! Hey!" Mark's got a goofy grin on his face. He's holding up a full-page drawing. It's a cartoon of mitochondria smoking cigarettes. The cell components are wearing blinging necklaces that bear their name. The mitochondria are surrounded by the rest of the cell parts. Like in a prison. In fact, the cell membrane is depicted as prison bars. The smoke is blended together. It wafts out the little window into the courtyard, where it forms a message that sits fat and dense across an obscured moon: *When Cell Respiration Goes Wrong.*

The bell rings. Mark snaps his book closed and takes his quiz up to Mrs. Didi. She smiles and waits by the door. I sit and stare at his seat. I look up. Sid's gone too. He usually waits for me. Mrs. Didi clickity-clacks her way down the row and stands by my side. She probably saw Mark's drawing. But she just hovers and doesn't say anything. I look her in the face. She lifts one of her penciled-on eyebrows. "Your quiz, Ed?" I fumble for the paper. End up wrinkling it before handing it off. Then I bend over. Zip up my bag. Almost have an accident. I make a beeline for the bathroom.

My hands shake and fumble as I unzip my fly. But I manage to whip it out without spilling. I fight the urge to sit down. Some things you just can't risk doing in school. I snap a quick glance at my reflection in the mirror while I wash my hands. My lips are cracked. I must have been licking them. I don't know how with the amount of time my tongue's been stuck to my palate. Maybe the poor sucker is afraid of my bottom teeth?

I walk out of the bathroom as the bell rings. I'm torn. There's a water fountain directly across from me. I'm so desperate for a drink that my mouth starts working in preparation. Like an infant's before she cries for the bottle. But to my right is my English classroom. Mr. Pilsner stands in the doorway. He's got his arms crossed and a slight grin on his lips. I look at him. Then at the water fountain. Then back. He narrows his eyes. Cocks his head to the left. Fortunately, someone starts yelling for him. Mr. P rolls into the classroom.

I lunge at the fountain and practically have a make-out session with it. I down roughly a glassful. I wipe my face with my sleeve and slide into class.

Mr. P is talking to Bob Homiller. Or rather, he's talking *at* Bob. Bob's nickname is "Silent Bob," after that guy from those stupid movies. He's always wearing some black wrestling or hardcore band shirt. Bob sits in the front of his classes and stares straight ahead.

Sid's in his regular seat. I want to crack something sarcastic. But my body just wants me to sit. I slump into my chair next to him.

"Where were you?" Sid doesn't look at me.

I was going to ask you the same damn thing. "Bathroom."

"Oh." He leans to me. Keeps looking across the room. He turns. His eyes glint like prisms. "Did you see Stacy?"

He says it like, "Did you *SEE* Stacy?"

What the hell kind of question is this? Of course I saw her. She draws attention like a fire alarm. I glance over. Oddly enough, she's looking at her reflection in a compact mirror. "Uh. Yeah. So?"

Sid snorts. "Well, you can't see it now. But she showed me in science." He pauses. I stare at him. "Her belly button. It's pierced." Sid's face scrunches when he says this. Like he's in pain. But then he smiles wide.

"Really?" I'm not at all surprised. Or truly care. I figure by the time Stacy's twenty, she'll have half of her body tattooed and piercings in places that only she'll be proud to talk about.

"Yeah. It's hot. Real hot." Sid takes another long look.

What's he thinking? Stacy's nothing but trouble. If he gets tangled up with her... Mr. P clears his throat. The telltale sign that the lecture is about to begin.

"Let us return to our foray with Shakespeare. Please take out your *Macbeth* books."

Same old nonsense. We started this play last class. It's all right. The action starts with these witches dancing around a cauldron. Mr. P actually asked Stacy and the dubious duo to play the parts. It worked out though. They got to wear black witch hats and skip in a circle, chanting: "Fair is foul, and foul is fair."

"Anyone remember how scene three ended?" Mr. P finds a spot in his book.

Kids look around. At their desks. At each other's rears. Not at Mr. P. No one answers.

"Macbeth is thinking about killing the king, and Banquo is warning him not to trust the witches."

The whole class looks at Mark. His book isn't even open. But his sketchbook is. Mr. P smiles. "Well done. That's absolutely correct." He looks over the rest of us. "Why is Macbeth thinking about killing King

Duncan?"

A smart girl up front raises her hand. "The witches' prophecies, and..." She pauses. "Well, really, because he believes the prophecies. Macbeth feels that he should be King. It's his fate."

The room's silent for a moment. Most kids look lost. Sid's staring at Stacy again. Pilsner clears his throat. "An excellent point. So let me ask, is fate real or imagined?" Mr. P likes to throw out these rhetorical questions. As he says, "just to put them out there and see what happens." Then he asks, "How much of your life do you control?"

❦

The bell rings and I awake in a puddle of drool. It's tough to open my eyes. I wipe up the drool with my book. Sid's not in his seat. I start packing up my stuff and hear laughter. I look up. The floozies are clumped together, pointing at me. "Nice forehead." Stacy touches her own. The three laugh like hyenas. Sid's with them. He laughs as well.

"What?"

"Your face is all red. You've got a big circle on your forehead." He presses the indentation.

I look down at my sleeve. Damn oversized buttons. I want to say something. To make a joke. Anything. But I can't get my brain to clear.

"Come on. We got P.E."

I stand and my bladder wakes up: *WE HAVE TO PISS!* I stumble up the row. I almost topple from the pain.

"Mr. Devlin, a word." Mr. P is standing at the end of the row. He's looking down his nose at me. Sid slaps me on the back. "Good luck." Uncomfortable reverberations torture my nether region. I want to cry.

"Enjoy your nap?"

I don't answer. I want this over ASAP.

"Well?" Mr. P uncrosses and then re-crosses his arms. "Fine. Finish reading scenes four and five, tonight."

I'm already nodding. I take a step before I realize he's not finished.

"As I was saying, catch up tonight." He pauses. "But really, Ed, are you okay?" His brow's furrowed. He seems sincere. "You haven't fallen asleep before..." He breaks off. Leans in. "I mean, you seem to enjoy English. Are you feeling all right?" He looks me over. "I have to admit, you don't look so great."

"I'm fine. Really."

"Okay then." He nods. I bolt.

I take a long, desperate piss. I don't give a damn if I'm late for P.E. I hold my lower back. Just cup it with my hand. It throbs from the strain. I finish and head to the sink. I watch the water plunge from the drain. I lower my head to drink. My weight slides with the water. My legs buckle under the effort to keep me upright. But now my head's spinning. I turn and the blue tile floor swallows me.

I smack the ground. I smell urinal cakes and stale piss. The bell rings above me. I'm on the bathroom floor. Not in P.E. I can't move. I can't speak. The hum of the bell dies away. My tongue becomes unglued from my mouth. I'm so thirsty that the blue of the tile is suddenly irresistible. My tongue probes out like a snail's foot. The tip touches the cold, wet tile. I swallow. Take a deep breath. Give it a full lick.

Chapter 2

Say from whence
You owe this strange intelligence or why
Upon this blasted heath you stop our way
With such prophetic greeting. Speak. I charge you. (1.3.78-81)

MRS. LEE, THE SCHOOL NURSE, COMES INTO FOCUS. Her tightly drawn eyes flutter behind razor-thin glasses. I try to sit up.

"No. Stay where you are." She pushes down on me. I stay put. She grabs a penlight and begins with the questions.

"Does your head hurt?"

I look up and back, as if I can actually see an injury. "No."

"What about your jaw? You landed on your chin."

I wiggle it and wince.

"I'll take that as painful." Mrs. Lee writes a note on a chart she has clamped to a clipboard. She rests it on her lap. She pops on the flashlight. "Let me have a look."

She has me open my mouth and move my tongue from side to side. She looks in my ears and in my nose. Then she leaves spots in my eyes. I squint them away. She gives me the prognosis.

"You may have cracked your jaw. You'll need an X-ray. But I'm sure that you don't have a concussion. You're lucky." She folds her hands on top of the clipboard. "Can you remember what happened?"

I look past Mrs. Lee, to the white privacy sheet that surrounds the cot I'm lying on. Then up at the drop ceiling. It is full of indentations and looks like tile. I want to spit. "I just went to the bathroom. Then felt really light headed. I fell down."

Mrs. Lee nods. "Number One or Number Two?"

It takes me a second to figure out her question. "Uh, Number One."

She nods. "Did anything hurt while you were urinating? Did you experience the fatigue while you were going?"

I lick my cracked lips. "No. I just went. Then I tried to get a drink from the sink." I pause and look at Mrs. Lee. "I'm always thirsty and always peeing."

A ripple of thought passes just beneath her glasses. "What do you mean?"

I feel stupid for speaking. But I know that now I've said it, she won't let it go. Like the time I took a softball below the belt. Mr. Martin, our P.E. teacher, sent me to Mrs. Lee. She questioned me for a solid fifteen minutes. Until I told her the truth: that my boys were red and ridiculously swollen. That I truly did not have a stomach ache. I turn away from her. "I don't know. Lately I've been going a lot. You know? At night. After every class."

"That often?"

"Yeah. I… uh… I'm thirsty all the time too. My mouth's like cotton." I don't mention the bathroom floor.

Mrs. Lee shifts in her chair and leans into me. She grips my wrist. It's cold. "Have you lost any weight recently?"

We used to have a scale in the bathroom. But my mom threw it out one day last winter. Something about her useless diet. "I don't know." I'm lying. I had to tighten my belt another hole this morning. My mom bought it in September.

Mrs. Lee hums a soft and barely audible sound. She then opens her mouth to speak, but a knock comes at the door.

"Mrs. Lee?" My mother's voice.

❧

I don't know what they're talking about. But I can get a read off my mom's expression. I'm headed to the hospital.

"So you're sure? No concussion?" My mom's hands are staked to her hips.

"Check for yourself." Mrs. Lee thrusts the flashlight forward.

My mom eyes it narrowly. Looks briefly at me. Shakes her head. "That's all right."

Mrs. Lee straightens. "There is one other issue, Mrs. Devlin." Her voice is soft.

My mom's face clears. As if she hadn't been paying attention. "Okay."

Mrs. Lee looks down at the chart on her lap. "Ed tells me that he's been urinating frequently."

My mom stares ahead, impassive.

"Also, he's finding it hard to quench his thirst." Mrs. Lee lets these two facts mingle before my mom. She stares ahead as if Mrs. Lee had told her that a ball is round and a box is square. Mrs. Lee turns to me. "How are you feeling, Ed?"

"All right. A little tired."

"Have you been more tired, recently? Like with the urinating? Is it more than normal?"

"Yeah. I just fell asleep in Pilsner's."

Mrs. Lee nods. She turns to my mom. "I can't be certain. Neither can Ed. But he looks like he's lost some weight."

My mom casts a look over me.

"I could give him a Keto-stick. Right now. If you'd like."

What the hell is a Keto-stick? Some kind of probe? My mom stares ahead. At some spot on the floor. I get goose bumps watching her. The way she looks now is the same way she did when she got the news that my Uncle Brian had been diagnosed with cancer. She hovered between our dinner and the living room. Unable to go one way or the other. My mom is in constant motion. Never inert. She even flops around while she sleeps. When she stands still, there's a reason.

Mrs. Lee fingers the corner of the clipboard.

After that phone call my mom collected herself, sat down in the living room, and stared at her hands. My father punched a hole in our kitchen wall when she told him. Now, my mom looks up. Her eyes glisten. "Thank you, but I don't think that will be necessary."

Mrs. Lee nods.

"I'll take him to Saint Mary's now."

❧

I know what it's like to be deaf. It's absolutely silent in my mom's car. Reminds me of that question about a tree falling in the forest. Mr. P brought that up one day. I thought it was the stupidest question with the most obvious answer. But now, I don't know. The silence is so heavy that I want to scream. But even if I do, I'm not sure my mom would hear me. She's got her hands glued to the wheel. Her eyes to the road. I turn to the window and stare. The landscape rolls along with us.

She pulls into the back lot at Saint Mary's—the one for employees—and parks her car. Like she's returning from lunch. She sets the emergency brake and sighs. I unhook and wait. She stares at the hospital for so long that I finally have to ask, "Am I all right?"

She answers by reaching out and stroking my hair. She smiles and bites back the sob blossoming in her throat.

We take the long route to the pediatric wing. Bypass the E.R. where she works. The pediatric waiting room is all cheery and painted bright yellow. Fuzzy Teddy bear pictures are mounted in oversized, multi-colored frames on the wall. There's a fish tank that bubbles in the corner next to a bin full of toys. I almost smile at how cute it all is. But then this little kid—probably three years old—stands on his chair. He's parked right next to the fish tank. Eyeballing the little suckers like he's going to try and grab one. Instead, he turns and taps his mom on the shoulder. She's got her head buried in some magazine. She takes a few seconds to respond. The little kid says, "Sick." Except it sounds like "Ick."

The mom looks at her son. Then at the tank. "Well don't touch the tank, honey. It's got yucky germs. Ick." She mimics, smiles, and returns to her magazine. The kid hovers there a second. His chubby little hands dance in the air. My mom goes to speak with the receptionist. I sit down across from him. His eyes bug. His mouth moves in that watery, loose-jaw way. I know what's coming. He puts one meaty hand on his mom's shoulder. Before she can comment, she's covered in alphabet soup and apple juice. The receptionist looks at the two and shakes her head. She leans to my mom. Pats her hand. She turns to the mom. "Don't worry, I'm calling a janitor." The bewildered mom does not respond. The kid looks a hell of a lot better. He turns to the fish tank and smiles. A line of undigested letters dots the front of his shirt.

My mom grabs a hold of my hand. "Come on."

She pulls me up. We walk down a long hallway. The floors gleam and reflect the fluorescent lights above. The air is antiseptic-laden. Has that… well… hospital smell. It's like blood and tissue, sweat and hair, and anxiety—if that has an odor. All boiled into an aroma that has the aftertaste of clothes starch.

My mom leads me into an examination room. I plop onto the bed. The white sterility paper crunches beneath me. I used to draw on the paper with crayons while Doc Stevens checked me over. He'd always tell me what a good artist I was. At the end of the exam he'd rip off the portion of the sheet I had drawn on. He'd say, "Frame it on your refrigerator." But I never did. My mom would throw the artwork out, saying, "Hospitals are filthy places."

Now she sits in a chair off to the side of the bed. I curl onto my side. I look at the cloud border and then up to the zoo animal mobile. It's just like it was when I was five. I chuckle and close my eyes.

֍

I awake to knocking at the door. I am utterly lost for an instant. My hand pumps in the air for the alarm clock. I sit up. Feel for the covers. I find my jeans and Doc Stevens walking into the room.

"Hey, Tiger." The door snaps closed behind Doc. He smiles that hey-even-though-you're-in-the-hospital-nothing's-wrong grin. *Who does he think he's fooling?* He darts past me and goes to my mom. "Kathy, how are you?" It's weird to hear Doc Stevens use my mom's name. Then again, they've known each other forever.

He turns to me. "So you smacked your chin in the bathroom?" He sits on one of those rolling chairs with the big squishy top. He's got a clipboard like Mrs. Lee's on his lap.

I try to smile. "Yeah."

"What, did someone leave a real nasty one in there and you passed out from the stench?"

I can't help but laugh out loud. So does Doc.

"Let me have a look." He scoots the chair over and puts his hands on my head. He twists and turns it. Makes little comments to himself. At one point I'm facing my mom. She doesn't look at me. She's staring off somewhere. Doc then pushes and pulls on my jaw. He has me open it wide. Asks if anything hurts or if anything is tender. Nothing is, so he places his hands on his knees with a slap. "Not broken!"

"Really?"

He cracks a gigantic smile. We both turn to my mom. She's still staring at the space before her. Doc coughs gently to bring her around.

"Oh. Okay. Are you sure?"

"Absolutely. I can send him for an X-ray if you'd like. But I'm certain it will reveal the same thing."

My mom shakes her head. "That won't be necessary." Then her face pulls. I remember the other reason we're here.

She adjusts in the seat. Her head is downcast. Her eyes are expectant. Doc leans to her. "I think we have a more serious issue." Her voice is a stitch above a whisper.

Doc looks between my mom and me. He speaks to my mom but looks at me. "Okay, go on."

My mom rehashes my symptoms: excessive thirst, excessive urination, lethargy, apparent dehydration, and rapid weight loss. *My God, I do sound sick.*

There's a moment of almost pure silence. The only sounds are the faint buzzing of the lights and Doc's measured breathing. He reaches out and touches my mom's hand. This is sad and comforting at the same time. While scary as all hell, too. If he's comforting her… then I'm… She looks up. He speaks. "We have to test him. For diabetes." My mom looks at me. A band of tears is wrapped into her eyelashes. Like the morning dew. She mouths her response. "I know."

Doc Stevens gets up, shoots me a hang-in-there-boy look, and pops out of the room. There isn't any more conversation. *What the hell? Is this serious, or just a cold? Maybe I'll get some antibiotics or something?* But my mom wouldn't be crying like she is now—her shoulders drawn up around her ears and her body quivering—if this was just some cold. Damn. If I'm sick. Like capital S.I.C.K. What the hell is my dad going to do with himself? Or with me?

Diabetes. "Die-a-bee-tees," I say to myself. It sounds like the beginning to one of those Japanese poems Mr. P. talked about. "Hi" something or other. *We die the bee tea.* Or, *We die from bee tea.* I picture this little Asian guy swirling a spoonful of bees into his tea. *What is wrong with me?*

I reach out to clasp my mom's shoulder. I mutter, "I'll be all right." She nods, but doesn't look at me. I withdraw my hand. *Dad should be here.* Then again, maybe not. I wonder if she'll call him. He's like a caged animal in a hospital. Always looking for an escape route. Because of my Uncle Brian. Despite how hard the doctors tried, they just couldn't come up with the answer. He died last New Year's Eve. After he died my mom and dad fought a lot about who should have done what and when. They haven't finished the argument. I don't think this will help.

Can diabetes kill you? The little Asian guy is laughing now.

The door opens. Doc Stevens's nurse Mindy walks in. She smiles and carries a gigantic syringe. My mom looks up. Sees her and the torture device. She winces.

"Hi, Ed, not feeling so good huh?" Mindy keeps smiling. She's not really asking. I shrug. "Well, I'm just going to take a little blood, so we can find out how to make you better."

They must teach this type of line somewhere, because it's completely illogical. I stare at my arms. "Which one?"

"Why don't you roll up your sleeves and we'll look." Mindy has on latex gloves. Her perky grin has taken on a sinister appearance.

My arms are like birch limbs. Pasty. White. Skinny. Yet my blue veins are visible, swimming just under the surface. Mindy taps the crook of my left arm and selects one of the veins that form a small "V" there. She takes rubber tubing and ties it around my bicep. *Heroin addicts.* I don't actually know any. I just saw a show on them. My veins bulge in an instant. I cannot understand why someone would willingly do what I know is coming next. I look at my mom. She nods once. Sharply.

I turn back and Mindy has the syringe before her. "It'll just be a quick pinch. That's it."

I smile. She wipes the vein with an alcohol pad. The smell stings my nostrils.

"Make a tight fist, Ed."

The needle is hot and makes me want to squirm. The metal pulses under my skin. The pressure builds at the puncture.

Mindy taps my hand. "Okay, open your fist."

The floodgate opens. My arm feels as if it's gushing. I don't want to look at it. But some sick and disturbed part of me forces me to. The blood pours out. It's deep maroon. It slowly fills the syringe's chamber. Mindy pulls on the plunger. My stomach slides with it.

The room spins. The walls blur. Shaking my head doesn't set them right again. Mindy's mumbling something. But her words blend in with the rest of the swirl. She places my right hand on top of my left arm. She wants me to apply pressure. This much I understand.

The room continues to whirl around me. I try to stand. I only succeed in crashing back onto the bed. The fluorescent lights play games with the happy, floating zoo creatures above. My heart quickens. My skin is moist with cold sweat. I try to focus. To hang on. But in a second, everything is gone.

Chapter 3

Your face... is a book where men
May read strange matters. To beguile the time,
Look like the time. Bear welcome in your eye,
Your hand, your tongue. Look like th' innocent
Flower. (1.5.73-77)

I AWAKE TO DOC STEVENS'S FACE. "There you are." He smiles. "Gave us a little scare." He places a wet cloth over my forehead. "How are you?"

I adjust my eyes. I'm cemented in place. My mouth is so dry it's arid. "I'm thirsty," I rasp.

Mindy comes into focus. She carries a cup with a straw. Her smile is gone. Her hands tremble while she holds the straw to my lips. I try to say, "Thank you," when I'm finished, but she retreats too quickly.

"You need to keep drinking." Doc frowns. "The dehydration. That's why you passed out." He pats my arm. "The test should take about an hour. Get some rest." He turns to my mom. "You too."

She looks haggard. Her mouth seems like it will never find a smile again. Her eyelids are puffy and sagging. Her eyes are thickly glazed like they were in the hallway last night. *Has it only been that long?* She nods at Doc's advice. Swipes a hand over her face. He squeezes my foot on his way out. "Hang in there, Tiger."

Sure, I'll just "hang." What the hell? Now it's just my mom, me, and one giant, unanswered question. I can almost see it. This absurdly

21

large question mark. Smoking a pipe. Wearing a know-it-all grin. He looks like Alex Trebek, the guy from *Jeopardy.* I bet Mark could draw it. Damn he has skills.

My mom sighs. Leans forward. Slowly stands up. She stretches and lets out a few grunts. Turns and casts a long-faced grimace. "You just try to rest. I'm going to go call your father."

I go to speak, but keep from doing so.

She notices. "What?"

I shake my head.

"What?" She tilts her head.

I can't say what I'm thinking. I point at the water. She fills the cup and hands it to me. "Thanks." She sets the cup by the sink when I'm finished.

"Okay, now?" She tussles my hair. It's a statement. Not a question.

I nod and roll on my side, as if to sleep.

"I'll be back in just a bit."

"Okay." She turns off the light. The door clicks softly. There's a shaft of light under the door. Shadows of feet emerge as people pass by. I can't sleep. I'm too scared and confused. About being sick. About what I almost said to my mom. *Don't call Dad. I don't want him here.* That would have been wrong. It would have sounded all snotty and full of I-hate-you emotion. That's not what I would have meant. What I *do* mean. What would have sounded right. Would have been, *Don't call Dad. I don't want to see what he thinks of me.*

The truth is my dad hates weakness. In turn, disease. It makes you weak. Cancer killed his brother. My unbelievably strong uncle. The shit hit the fan the day he realized Brian wasn't going to pull through. He ripped a door off its hinges at the hospital. But I'm already weak. Always have been. I know my dad's ashamed of this. *How in God's name am I going to make him proud, now?*

I don't know what I'm going to do. I hop off the table and flip on the light. I brought my backpack in with me. Just habit I guess. I pull out *Macbeth.* I need diversion. It's all I've got. I start reading scene four.

Looks like Macbeth is going to be king. Even his wife believes it's his destiny. Which she says she'll help him achieve by getting all "unsexed." Creepy. I close the book. The door opens.

"School work?" My mom steps into the room and sits.

"Yeah, all finished." I go to my bag and put *Macbeth* away. She watches me when I stand. Like she wants to say something. But the door opens. Doc returns.

He's got a yellow sheet of paper in his hand. He shoots me a weak grin and then whispers to my mom. I sit back on the exam bed. *Here we go.*

He turns to me. "Want a drink?"

I nod. He grabs my cup and refills it at the sink. My mom is wiping tears with her fingertips. I take the water. The cold against my palm is refreshing. I was beginning to feel like a swollen hot dog. I drink and Doc begins.

"Ed, I've got your test results." He lets the sentence hang in the air. "But your mom wants to explain it to you."

My mom clears her throat. She sits upright and wipes another batch of tears. "Honey. You have type one diabetes." She waits. So do I. "Do you know what that means?"

I shrug. "I'm sick?"

"Yes, but it's not like a cold or the flu." She pauses. "You have a *disease.*"

Ok, so now what? I stare at them. They look at each other. Then at me. They want me to speak. That's obvious. But what do I say?

"What your mom is saying is that your sickness won't just go away."

I crinkle my forehead. "I'm going to be like *this*, forever."

Doc shakes his head. "Not quite so." He looks at the floor for a second. "You're sick now. In a different way from how you will *always* be sick. Right now is the worst stage."

I'll always be sick?

"Right now you are sick because your body isn't making something that you need. Once you get that *something* then you will feel better. But you won't be cured." He looks at my mom. She's nodding. He continues.

"You will *always* need what your body isn't naturally producing. You will have to get it artificially."

My head's swimming. This feels like science class. I don't understand. I don't care. I just want to go home. But I know I have to ask, "What am I missing?"

"Insulin. Your body isn't making any insulin," my mom says.

"Why?"

My mom leans in. "Well, it's complicated. Sometimes children get sick, and then their pancreases just stop working."

"Why do they *stop*?" My voice cracks.

Doc Stevens pats my knee. "You got sick. For some reason your body got confused and sent out the wrong message. It told your immune system to attack your pancreas. That's the organ that makes insulin."

"And now it doesn't work?"

Doc and my mom nod.

What's the big deal? From what I remember my appendix doesn't work either. Nobody's does. We all seem to be getting along just fine. I shift on the bed. The familiar pressure in my bladder sloshes from side to side. "So then all I have to do is take some insulin and I'm all set?"

My mom and Doc have the same facial expression that my teachers get when they have to mold an answer I've given.

"Not quite so." Doc cocks his head. "Let me explain."

The explanation is over. My mom's staring at me as if I might collapse again. I'm ordering all that Doc has said into my own words:

I need the insulin I don't have in order to live.

Insulin is what helps the body use the carbohydrate we eat.

The carbs are turned into sugar. Insulin comes along and moves the sugar for energy. Or stores it for use later.

Without insulin all this sugar just floats around because the insulin isn't there to transport it to where it needs to go. Kind of like people who can't hail a taxi.

If this sugar is just left floating around for long enough it causes all sorts of problems. Like the ones I've had: excessive thirst, urination, dehydration, fatigue.

If it continues to hang around, this extra sugar screws up the organs. It binds to this protein on blood cells and then clogs up organs. Like kidneys. Decreases circulation all around. This can lead to amputations. If this goes on long enough without detection, death. Plain and simple. I'd be dead without medical treatment. I can't go on living without insulin.

There is no doubt that this is not going to go over well with my dad.

I stare at the floor. Doc coughs. "The main part of this disease is balancing." His hands are up in the air like a scale. "You've have to eat really healthy, and take the right amount of insulin for the healthy carbs you do eat."

"Sounds like fun."

Doc frowns. "It's tough." He leans in. "But you've got one hell of a mom to help you."

I look at my mom. *Is he seeing what I am?* She looks like a broken piece of furniture that's been left out by the side of the road.

He continues. "You should also get into exercising. It helps maintain blood sugar levels. I know your dad works out. He could help."

I laugh. I don't mean to. My ears redden. Doc lifts an eyebrow. My mother turns away. "I'll talk to him."

"Good. Because you want to avoid high and low blood sugars—Hyper and Hypoglycemia. A normal level is between 80 and 120." He makes a line with his hands. Then shoots one up toward the ceiling. "When your sugar level is high—let's say over 200—that's hyperglycemia. This will happen if you eat a lot and don't take the right dose of insulin. Or eat too much. You'll feel like you do now. Have to pee a lot. Really thirsty. If you get really high—like over 800—you could go into a coma and die."

I clench my jaw.

Doc lowers his hand to his knee. "If you go low. Say under 75. That's hypoglycemia. This will happen if you take too much insulin.

You'll also get this way if you exercise and haven't eaten enough carbs. You haven't felt this, yet."

I swallow. *There's more?* "What's it like?"

"Shaky, irritable, confused. You'll break out into a cold sweat. You might get really tired or hungry." Doc leans into me. "If you don't eat some quick-acting carbs. Like candy. Or drink some juice. You'll pass out. If that happens and you don't get help. You could go into a coma and could die."

My head throbs. My ears ring. It's as if I've just come out of a concert. I rub a hand over my forehead. "I have to pee."

The air in the hallway is refreshing, in spite of the antiseptic aroma. I walk to the bathroom. It's like I've got a water balloon sewed inside me. The clock at the end of the hallway displays 2:15. I'd just about be done with my day at school. I'd be in math with Mrs. Haight. Probably cracking jokes with Sid. Then again, maybe not. Sid's probably planning a rendezvous with Stacy. Would be regardless of my presence.

I head back to the exam room, feeling ten pounds lighter. Doc is filling a syringe with a clear liquid. He turns and smiles. "Lesson One, injections."

Needles?

"Let me ask you a question, Ed. Sort of a pop quiz. First, hop on the bed."

I do. "All right." I try not to stare at the syringe.

"What is a normal sugar level?"

I close my eyes and see Doc balancing his hands. "Between 80 and 120."

"Excellent!" My mom bounces in her chair. She's smiling.

"Now, a guess." Doc strokes his chin. "What do you suppose your sugar level was?"

Is he's getting some sort of sick pleasure out of this? What the hell? "Four hundred."

Doc shakes his head. "Sorry, Charlie. Higher."

"Higher?" My mom's voice quavers.

Doc looks at her and nods. He turns back to me. "Your level was 648."

This number juts out like an egg-shaped bruise. I do the math. I'm 528 "somethings" off the mark. *Jesus!*

"You got lucky, Ed. Most people would be incredibly sick. Possibly in a coma at such a level." He turns to my mother. "We'll get you straight." Doc's voice has softened. "That's where this comes in." He holds out the syringe.

"Insulin?"

"Yup, your new best friend. Your sugar level will be normal in no time." He holds an opened alcohol pad now. I roll up my sleeve and wait. "Not there. Your abdomen."

I pull up my shirt and tuck it under my chin. Doc applies the alcohol and says something about why the belly is the best place to inject. But I'm not listening. The room is starting to swirl again.

"Just a quick pinch." He teases a fold of my skin between his fingers. "On three."

I close my eyes.

"One."

My skin is cold. My belly has goose bumps.

"Two."

My heart bangs in my ears. I hold my breath.

"Three."

The needle punches through my skin. I'm on fire. But I don't flinch because I cannot imagine how much *that* would hurt. Doc's murmuring something in my ear. It's drowned out by my racing heart. The insulin courses under my skin. It spreads out. My stomach flips. One bead of cold sweat runs down my back.

"All set."

I open my eyes. He's holding the now-empty syringe before him. I look from it to my belly. There's a small red welt on it. The insulin tingles as it settles. My head swims. The room spins. My stomach does another back flip. I go to speak, but end up crashing onto the bed.

The room winks. My mom's biting her fingernails. Her eyes dart like trapped flies. Doc bends to my ear. "Just breathe. Relax and breathe." I close my eyes and listen to my heart. It slows after a while. I look again.

"Better?" Doc hands small white sheets of paper to my mom.

"Yeah." I sit up.

"Ready to go home, then?"

I don't answer. My mom does. "We're ready."

Hold up! Home? Now? I expected to be here for a week after Doc's explanation. Now I'm going *home* with these papers and my mom? I'm supposed to be fine? I want to hand the prescriptions back. Refuse to take them. Do something. But I don't. I slide to the end of the bed and stand up. I'm not feeling light-headed anymore. Instead, I'm absolutely petrified.

"Have you scheduled another appointment?" Doc grabs the door handle.

"Friday." My mom tucks the prescriptions in her purse.

"Good. But feel free to come in or call before then. You know my schedule."

My mom nods.

"Okay then, let me walk you out."

I leave the room first. We reach the waiting room and the little kid with his puke is gone. A little girl is seated next to her mom in place of him. She stares at the fish while her mom reads a paperback book.

"Feel better, Ed. I'll see you Friday." Doc ruffles my hair. He turns to my mom. "If you need anything…"

"Absolutely. Thank you."

Doc smiles in response. We walk wordlessly to the car. A deep orange is beginning to flood the horizon. Streetlights are popping on. I get in the car and buckle my seatbelt. It's the only sense of security I feel.

Chapter 4

But here, upon this bank and shoal of time,
We'd jump the life to come. But in these cases
We still have judgment here, that we but teach
Bloody instructions, which being taught, return
To plague th' inventor. (1.7.6-10)

WHAT DOESN'T CVS/PHARMACY HAVE that you could possibly want? Aisle nine offers cat food and pens. Maybe I'll pick up a can of cat food. A package of pens. A pair of pantyhose. Then I'll just go have a wacky-good time for myself. I admit I'm getting a little slaphappy. But I've been pacing the store for almost an hour. My mom gave my prescriptions to the pharmacist—this chick who looks my age. She even has braces. I was told to go wander because my mom had to make some calls. It's no wonder that I'm having crazy, cat-lady thoughts.

"Ed, come here." My mom's standing near the checkout counter. Waving me over to her. Some poor old guy is leaning into the consultation area. He yells at the top of his lungs.

"I need my pills. I've been backed up for days."

I go to my mom. "You've got to pick out one of these." She points at a shelf. The pharmacist tells the old guy it'll be another five minutes. Then she directs him to the aisle with the ex-lax. I refocus and see what my mom is talking about.

For a moment it's like I'm a little kid standing in the aisle of Toys "R"

Us. She's pointing at a wall display of little gadgets I've never seen before. They look like some kind of cell phone. But I'm in CVS. Yes, they have a lot, but these have to be related to my new disease. "What are they?"

"Glucose monitors. You test your sugar level with them." She squats down to get a closer look.

My face flushes. I look out of the corners of my eyes to see if anyone is looking at me. But the place is filled with old farts who can't hear an ambulance siren and scream about their bowels. I'm in the clear. I join my mother.

The monitors mostly look the same: small plastic devices, with large display screens and a couple of squishy black buttons on them. I flip down a couple of the boxes and read the backs. They all talk about "accurate blood glucose results in just seconds." My mom nudges me. She's holding a slim monitor, roughly the size of my thumb.

"A lot of the patients I see use this one." She pushes the box into my hands. I look it over and feel her watching me. It's like Christmas. Damnit. I'd better like this new toy. "It's quick and small. Easy for carrying. It will even fit into your jeans."

Does she have any idea how that just sounded? I hand the box over. "All right."

"Are you sure?"

I shrug. I just want this pick-your-new-best-friend-male-organ-laced conversation to be over. She stands and heads to the register. Two white bags with "Devlin" scrawled across them sit on the counter. One is filled with prescriptions. The other is filled with supplies that my mom picked up. She's been real busy while I've been thinking about cat food and the pharmacist. The braces-girl takes the box from my mom. "Good choice." She punctuates with a metallic grin. I have nothing to say in return, so I stare at my feet. The pharmacist turns to my mom. "I'll just run this through. Get the strips for it. You'll be all set."

All set, my ass. I chuckle. My mom gives me that not-now look. I walk over to the aisle that sells adult diapers to see if I can find the old guy getting prepared for an explosion.

~୧୨~

We pull into the driveway. Dad's truck is not here. Instant relief. Hopefully like it will be for that old guy. I'm tired. I just want to go to bed. It's only 5:00 but it feels like midnight.

The house has that closed-up, stale quality. Something about the light and the air. My mom grabs me by my shoulders. "Go sleep. I'll wake you up for dinner." I'm pulled toward my room as if by the sheer gravity of my exhaustion. I don't even take my jacket off before I lie down on top of my comforter.

I snap awake when my mom strokes my cheek. I can see only her silhouette. The light in the hall illuminates behind her. My room is night-time blue. "You okay?" It takes me a second to understand this question. To realize just where I am, and why. I roll over.

She doesn't say anything about my jacket. "Your father's home." She looks at the floor. "I'll have dinner ready in a half hour."

"Great."

My mom stands. "Come out when you're ready."

What if I never am?

~୧୨~

I use the bathroom before I head to the kitchen. I still look like crap. My piss still smells like garbage. The TV blares from down the hall. I brace myself for the encounter.

I walk into the kitchen and my dad looks up from the tube. My heartbeat is vibrating my shirt.

"Hey."

"Hey, Dad." I'm frozen in place. My mom is stirring something in a pot behind my dad. She sets the spoon down on the stove and I jump at the sound. My father leans in and turns off the TV. This is monumental. I mean, it's 6:30. The "friggin' highlights" are on.

"Have a seat."

I sit down like a zombie. But my brain's running on overdrive: *Does he know? He must know! What did my mom tell him? What did he say? What did he do?* My heart still thrums. I wait for the talk. The man-to-man encounter. He clears his throat. He clears it again. He shifts in his seat. His eyes keep drifting to the right. He can't look me in the face. I wait. He starts. Opens his mouth. Looks to his right. Then back. Says nothing. I turn to see what's got him so worked up.

The typical items are on the table: plates, bowls, cups, silverware. But also, on the far end are my monitor, syringes, alcohol pads, a couple of bottles of insulin, some books, and a mess of other tubes and medical-looking products. My Uncle Brian's room looked just like this. Medical crap everywhere.

My mom crosses the room and stands behind my father. "Well, here we go." She forces a smile.

I don't say anything because my voice is now caught in my throat. It stings like I've swallowed a razor blade.

My mom moves to the end of the table. "I figured we'd all learn about this big change *together*." She picks up my monitor and a red, biohazard container. She walks to me. "I know Doc Stevens talked about your sugar level. But he didn't go into how you actually test it."

"Okay." My voice sounds as strong as lettuce.

She sits down next to me and places the container on the table. "You have to check your level in the morning. Before lunch. After lunch. Before and after dinner. Before you go to bed. Also any time you don't quite feel right."

Like now? "Sure."

My mom smiles and unzips my monitor. It looks exactly like it did on the box. But in addition there's a little cylinder and a pen-like thing. "Let me show you how this works. Then you'll test. We'll get the result. You'll take your insulin. Then we can eat."

And then what? "All right."

My mom pulls a little strip of plastic from the cylinder. "This is a test strip." She inserts it into the meter, turning it on. She then picks up the pen thing and pops the top off. It's hollow inside. A chamber in the base. My mom reaches into a box and she pulls out this plastic piece that is almost like a Lego. "A lancet." She sticks this thing into the pen's chamber. Twists off the circular tab on top. A miniscule needle glistens under the light.

My dad shifts uncomfortably in his seat.

My mom screws the top back onto the pen thing. She pulls back a little lever on it. "Now, give me one of your fingers." She extends her hands.

I look from her to my father. Her eyes are soft and pleading. His are bugging out of his head. I thrust my pinkie forward.

"You'll hear a pop but won't feel a thing." My mom first wipes my finger with an alcohol pad. "Ready?" She places the pen thing's tip against the pad of my pinkie. I breathe in. My father grinds his teeth.

The sound is like one of those toy guns that fire suction cup darts. The pen bangs out. A quick sting follows. But it hurts a lot less than I imagined. A droplet of blood appears on my finger.

"Squeeze just below it."

I do. The blood pools.

"Good. Now move your hand and put the blood on the tip of the strip."

I rotate my hand. The blood slides. I snap my hand back. The blood flies off and lands on my dinner plate. "Damn."

My dad backs up his chair.

"Just try again," my mom says.

This time I rotate my hand, squeeze, and successfully get the blood onto the strip. My mom smiles and hands me the alcohol pad to wipe up the blood. I look at my meter. Fat numbers count back from five. The meter beeps. I'm holding my breath. 375 sits on the screen.

My mom hands me a little white book and a pen. "Open it up and write down your result."

I flip open the cover. It's a bunch of blank charts. There's a box for glucose readings. Another for grams of carbohydrate. Another for the amount of insulin. There's even a little space for comments. I write "375" and "6:15 PM." I leave the comment section blank.

"Now, your insulin." My mom's already got a vial out of its box.

"Here, you do it." She hands me the vial, a syringe and an alcohol pad. My dad looks to the food on the stove. To me. Then to my mom. Finally, somewhere off in the distance.

"Check your coverage sheet first." She slides it to me.

Doc gave my mom this little graph that indicates how much extra insulin I need to take for high readings. I find the 350-375 range. "Five units."

"Good. Now what?"

"I have no idea." My voice catches.

"Insulin for dinner."

I look down. My head is sluggish. "How much?"

"Forty-five grams of carb."

I stare at the insulin and syringe. "So how much?"

My father shakes his head in a "you're an idiot" kind of gesture.

"You take one unit of insulin for every fifteen grams of carbohydrate." My mom waits for me to do the calculation.

"Three units."

"Plus?"

"Right. Five for the high. That's eight total."

"Exactly. Go for it."

I wipe off the top of the insulin with the alcohol pad. Then I grab the syringe. I pull off the orange cap. Pull the plunger back to the number five. Then farther to the third black hash mark after. I push the needle through the rubber center of the vial's top. I push the plunger down. Hold the vial. Flip it over. The plunger pops back like on a trigger. It fills with the clear liquid.

My father's watching me. His jaw's working overtime.

The plunger levels with eight units. I pull the syringe out. I tease up my shirt and stare at my white belly. The red dot from earlier is still there. Like a pimple. I grab the alcohol pad. Wipe down a patch of skin on the opposite side. The alcohol is cold and wet. Like an ice cube's kiss.

Chair legs scrape across the floor. "I can't watch this." My dad stands. He looks unsteady on his feet. We lock eyes. It's awful. Even worse than my mom at 3 AM. His eyes are swimming in his head. He bolts to the stove and places his hands on the counter. He keeps his back to us. A tear smacks my side. I won't let the rest go until I finish. I pinch the skin, and quickly, without thinking, without waiting, slam the needle in. It burns and then pulsates deep within. My head is instantly on fire. But I steady the base of the needle and push in the insulin. The same seeping sensation enters. I bite my lower lip. I push the plunger to the bottom. Pull the needle out. Sit back. My mom is crying. So am I. She reaches across the table and hands me another alcohol pad. I take it. But make no use of it. Instead I look at my father. He's still at the counter. I want to scream. To cry harder. To throw something against the wall. I place my syringe in the biohazard container. My father unwilling to look at me. My abdomen and finger are clotting their new wounds. My mom stands. "I'll get dinner."

✎✎✎

My mom tucked me into bed a while ago and told me that I don't have to go to school tomorrow. Possibly for the rest of the week. I've just been staring at the wall. My brain's whirring. I figured reading would help me sleep, so I read some more *Macbeth*. Act One, scenes six and seven.

Macbeth decides he doesn't want to kill the king after all. But then his wife totally disses him. Asking if he's afraid of his fate and if he's truly a man. There's one nasty chick. Macbeth changes his mind back. Probably a good idea, for his sake. Lady Macbeth's no joke.

But my brain just won't settle. I shift and my bladder cries for relief.

I shuffle out of my room and into the hall. The house is dark except for my parents' room. A shaft of light shines from beneath their door. It's closed. I don't remember a time when they've closed their door. It's like that policy—our policy on foreigners—the "Open Door Policy." They've always been available to me. Not tonight.

Sharp murmurs slide out. Just like the conversations they had right after Uncle Brian died.

I step past the door and walk into the bathroom. I don't bother with

35

the light. I step through my dad's gritty shavings. Like sawdust under my feet. I sit down on the toilet and picture Sid's bathroom. Which makes me think of Sid. *What in the hell am I going to say to him?*

A lock clicks against doorjamb. The "hoosh" of door across carpet follows. My father's got a pillow under his arm. He closes the door to his bedroom behind him. Stands before it. He sighs and pulls a hand across his face. Over his head. To the back of his neck. It's as if he's trying to realign his thoughts.

I sit on the toilet watching him. I do not breathe. I pray he doesn't have to piss. I wait. In a moment he walks by. When I finish I do not flush the toilet nor do I run the water. I tiptoe into the hall and freeze. The silence swims in currents around me. My dad is settled in the recliner. My mom is in her room. Now dark.

I return to my room and close the door. I lie back in bed and stare out the window. He's been up like this for a while now. I don't know exactly how long. But with all my nighttime pissing I've seen him a lot. Just staring at the TV. He used to sleep well. I used to have to go in and jump on his bed to wake him. Not anymore. Not since... last year.

I roll over and stare at the ocean wallpaper. That doesn't help. I don't want to think anymore. Not about my dad. Or my dead uncle. Or my disease. Just last night I wanted to know why I was pissing so much. Now I do. What good has it done?

Chapter 5

Mine eyes are made the fools o' th' other senses
Or else worth all the rest. (2.1.56-57)

"Ed." MY MOM NUDGES MY SHOULDER. "Ed, wake up. You have to test and take your shot." I roll over. Look at the clock. It's 7 AM. I'm exhausted. But I was only up twice during the night. Both times my father was bathed in the blue light of the television. I sit up. Yesterday comes flooding back in fragmented pieces. A puzzle I'm just waking up to reassemble. My mom's holding my meter in her hands. I remember what to do and test. This time without flicking blood everywhere. The meter beeps: 415.

"It's okay." My mom removes the strip, shutting the meter off. "You haven't had any of the Lantus yet. That will help.

My brain tries to locate *that* word. It comes up empty. I give her a blank look. She holds up an insulin vial. "This is the long-acting insulin you take only in the morning."

"Right." I give a little click of my tongue to show that I knew all along.

My mom doesn't buy the charade. "You can't mix this in the same syringe with your other insulin." She holds up two syringes before setting them on the nightstand next to me. "Check your coverage sheet for the Humalog. The Lantus will always be 18 units."

I check the sheet and do the computation. "Which one first?"

"Humalog."

I grab an alcohol pad, a syringe and the insulin. I draw up six units and let the vial fall to my lap. I pull up my shirt and inject as quickly as I can. The insulin still kicks under my skin. At least my other injection sites seem to be disappearing. I repeat the process with the Lantus. I've got two vials of insulin, two syringes, and two used alcohol pads in my lap. I look like a junkie.

My mom reaches down and pulls another biohazard container from yet another plastic pharmacy bag. She plops it down on my nightstand. "This one will stay in here."

I plop my syringes into the container. They clack like crayons in a large bin. A thought slaps me upside the head: *My insulin for breakfast?* "What about breakfast? I didn't take any..."

"It's all right. You're not eating now. Your level is too high. We'll wait until it comes down to a more appropriate level." She pats my hand. "You can go back to sleep. I'll get you in a couple of hours."

My mom leaves. I pull my covers up around my head. My parents are speaking low, almost inaudibly, out in the hall. I pull back the covers. I strain to hear, but the words are still lost. I take in my room: the alcohol pads and syringes on my desk. The biohazard container my test kit on the nightstand. I frown and pull the covers back over my face.

I snap awake. Like a sprung trap. My mom recoils from me. I'm covered in sweat. I kick off the covers. My mom stands and watches. "I'm hungry."

She laughs. "I thought you might be." She motions with her head to my nightstand. "Test. Then go eat."

I grab my meter and slide a strip out of the bottle and into place. I pick a spot on my middle finger. Wipe it with alcohol. Hold my breath. I get the blood onto the strip and in five seconds have the result: 150. It's like seeing an A-. It isn't perfect. But after all the Fs, I'll take it.

"All right! Write down that and the results from earlier." She messes my hair. "You're getting better already."

I fill in my logbook and then head toward the kitchen.

"Grrrrr!"

What the...?

"Grrrrrr!"

My stomach is screaming at me. It drags me into the kitchen and flings me into a chair. My mom's got a sweet spread on the table: buttered toast, scrambled eggs with cheese, bacon and sausage. It's like a Denny's commercial. I dive in.

I'm stuffed and my plate looks brand new. I lean back in my chair.

"So, how many carbs did you eat?"

It's like she's snapped a rubber band against my forehead. I have no idea: *a couple slices of toast. A small glass of OJ. Four or five links. A handful of bacon. A ton of eggs with ketchup.* I shrug.

My mom tsks. "You've got to keep track. That's why I didn't remind you before you started. You eat a meal like that without taking your shot, and bang, you're up in the 300s."

I stare at my empty plate and feel like it. "I know it's rough. But here are the labels. Figure it out." My mom slides the bread loaf, the sausage and bacon packets, the OJ container, the ketchup bottle, egg carton, and cheese package across the table. I read the labels like those people who stand in the grocery store muttering to themselves about fat content.

I add up 55 grams of carbohydrate. I grab the coverage chart that my mom has conveniently left near my plate. I need one unit to cover my 150 reading. *But what's my ratio?* "What's my ratio?"

My mom doesn't look up from the counter where she's flipping through a *Better Homes and Gardens* magazine. "One to fifteen."

I take my shot. My mom pretends not to watch. I play along. When I'm through she kisses the top of my head. "We're going to visit your grandfather this morning. Sid's coming over after school."

"How did...why are we...what the?"

"No point in sitting around. Your grandfather wants to see you. We don't visit enough as is. Sid's bringing your homework. I called the school yesterday and arranged it." She pauses. "Ed, you'll have a lot of support." She squeezes my shoulder and then walks to the sink.

I sit while she does the dishes and think about my conversation with Sid. This is big. I have to prepare. However, no matter how I envision the encounter—cracking jokes or showing him all my medical stuff—his face is the same, lost. Unfortunately, I also imagine him telling Stacy, and she in turn, her minions. This scenario reminds me of some teen slasher film, with kids running around screaming and falling down: *No! Not DIABETES! Ahhhhhh!* I stand to leave the table. I bump the chair and it scrapes across the floor. It reminds me of my father's reaction the night before. My stomach drops. The food I just ate bounces heavily.

I go to my room. Might as well kill some time before going to see Gramps. I pick up Macbeth and find Act Two, scene one.

Macbeth trips out and asks a floating dagger if he's supposed to kill the king. *Or is it just his conscience?* Maybe Lady Macbeth was right. Maybe he is afraid of doing what he has to in order to succeed.

I can't imagine living to be as old as these people. It's a frightening, frightening proposition. We're in the lobby of my grandfather's "retirement village," crossing to the receptionist's desk. Visitors have to check in first in order to see whether or not the old fart still remembers who he is and isn't about to throw his dentures across the room.

I stare at a guy who is in a wheelchair with a giant tray. It's like a high chair for infants. All that is on his tray is a puddle of drool fed by a shoestring-thick strand that hangs from the corner of his down-turned mouth. He's got these vacant eyes. Like my mom gets. He doesn't see the drool or his hands playing in it. Hell, he probably doesn't even see the village around him. I have to turn away.

"Yes, your father is expecting you." The receptionist smiles. "I'll call his room and let him know you're here."

A minute later Gramps is walking down the hallway. *He* doesn't need any assistance. In fact, he moves better than some of the orderlies. He gives a little wave to his friends, and then patters over to us.

"Sweetheart." He kisses my mom on the cheek. They separate.

"Hey, Dad. How are you feeling?"

Gramps smiles, clears his throat. "Like a sailor with a weekend pass. These ladies better watch out." He cackles. A laugh seasoned with poker nights, cigars and whiskey.

"But hey!" He turns to me. "How about you? I hear you've got a touch of the sugar."

"Uh…" I have no idea what to say. *Is this some weird old fart slang for diabetes?*

"Yes, Dad." She touches his arm. "He has *diabetes*."

"Oh you make it sound so serious, Dear. Ed, you feeling okay?"

"Yeah." Obviously that's what he wants to hear.

"Good. Stay that way." He motions around the room. "Half the people in here got *die-a-bee-tus*. They're still trucking."

My earlier thought is solidified: *No, I definitely don't want to live this long.*

My mom sighs and looks over her shoulder.

"What. What is it, Sunshine?" Gramps' voice is on the verge of baby talk. My mom looks at him and tries not to laugh. "You are my sunshine, my only sunshine. You make me happy, when skies are gray…" Gramps sings.

Mom laughs and leans into him. "Stop, stop. I'm fine. Let's go out to the courtyard."

Gramps claps his hands. "I like your thinking."

The courtyard is actually pretty cool. It's got park benches everywhere because old people always have to sit. But it's also got shuffleboard and tennis courts. A little garden path—complete with a stream—runs under a wooden plank bridge. There are blobs of old people in pastel outfits walking to various buildings and recreation areas. Out here it truly looks like a village. We sit on a bench near the stream.

Gramps clears his throat. "Ed, I'm glad you came. I don't see enough of you. And I wanted to make sure that you were made of some O'Reilly blood. Not just Devlin."

I give him a goofy, I-don't-know-what-the-hell-you're-saying grin.

41

"We O'Reillys are strong people. It'll take more than a silly disease like diabetes, or cancer—bless your grandmother's soul—to take us down." He pauses for a moment. "You seem just fine. That lets me know you'll pull through."

"Thanks."

"You're welcome, boy." He slaps me on the leg. "You got shots and that damn little prick test?"

My mom's eyes widen. " I… Uh. Yeah."

"Son-of-a-bitch stuff! My friend Earl's got the *die-a-bee-tus*. No shots for him. Just pills. But he's always pricking his damn finger, though." Gramps imitates the lancet with his index finger. "Nasty when he plays cards with us. Sometimes he hasn't finished bleeding when he picks up." Gramps chuckles. "It's all right though. His cards always suck. He sort of marks them for us." I feel sorry for Earl. Even though I've never met him.

❧

Everything's fuzzy. I follow my mom up the back steps. Stumble. I right myself on the railing. I drag myself up the stairs behind her. She's putting the key in the lock. Taking forever. I'm hot. Need to sit down. "Come on!" My voice is deep. Drags itself from inside of me with much effort.

My mom shoots me a look. This penetrating glance from under her eyelids. She unlocks the door. I fall in step behind her. I don't get far. She whirls around on me. "Sit down!" She pulls my wrist toward the kitchen table. I wrench it away.

"I got it!" I sit at the table and pull off my jacket. I get caught in the sleeves. I slip loose and just hurl the damn thing on the floor. My mom picks it up and fishes my kit out of it. She places it on the table before me. Walks to the fridge.

I don't want to test! I grab it to fling it away. But I pause, mid-toss. My hand is shaking. My meter falls to the table. My stomach grinds to life. I wipe sweat from my forehead. My skin is clammy. I'm pissed off and hungry. Everything around me is either too loud or too hot. Just too much. I peel open my test kit and thump around with my wobbly hands. The screen rolls back and then displays the reading: 56. Something moves on my right. My mom hands me a juice box. I try to take it from her. But I'm like a runner unable to take the baton. She holds the straw to my lips. Looks down at the monitor. "Whew! Just what I thought."

The juice is sunshine in my mouth. My mom sits next to me and pats the back of my hand. I'm sickened by the way her palm sticks to me. "You'll be fine. Just give it a few minutes."

The waves of noise subside in my head. Like I've taken off earbuds to an iPod. The room is less offensive. My skin is no longer melting. "I'm sorry."

My mom looks at me like a puppy. Her cocked head and wrinkled brow. "For what?"

"Yelling at you," I mumble.

She leans in. Puts her other hand on my forearm. "Listen honey, it's not your fault. No one can blame you for that. It's not under your control." My mom reaches up and runs a finger over the skin just above my ear. "Do you remember what hemophilia is?"

I shrug.

"That's the disease your friend Danny—remember him from first grade—that's what he had."

I remember Danny. He was this goofy little freckled kid with pumpkin-colored hair. When we played he'd say he had to "be careful." I nod.

"Well, if you remember, you always had to be careful around him. That's because he had hemophilia. If he got cut, he couldn't stop bleeding. *His* body didn't have what it needed to clot." My mom stares at me for a moment. "Would you be angry with Danny if he got cut and couldn't make a scab?"

"That's stupid."

"Exactly. So how can I get upset with you? It's not like you *tried* to get angry. Your body was just reacting to the lack of sugar in your system. It was forcing you to make a scene and get help."

This is some weird-ass logic. But what do I know? "All right. I get it."

"Good." She pats me on the hand. Most of the clamminess is gone. The fog around the room is beginning to lift.

Chapter 6

Will all great Neptune's ocean wash this blood
Clean from my hand? No, this my hand will rather
The multitudinous seas incarnadine,
Making the green one red. (2.2.78-81)

IT'S 3:30. MY RUG IS VACUUMED. My bookshelves are straightened. My desk has a discernable surface. My computer no longer looks like a deep-sea creature blindly finding its way through the abyss. My bed is no longer a twisted mass of blankets, sweat and turmoil. My mom should be pleased.

It was her idea for me to clean my room. I was 185 before lunch. Instead of having me take insulin to cover the high, she suggested this toil. Because cleaning—especially how much I had to do—is like exercise. The natural way to bring a sugar level down. It made me nervous though. Because I don't want go low again. Ever.

I sit and find Act Two, scene two of *Macbeth*.

If *CSI* were around way back in medieval times—when the play takes place—Macbeth would have been done. Blood is hard to disguise, and people always have questions when it's been spilled. Macbeth screwed up while killing the king. Needed Lady Macbeth to finish the job. Therefore they both got bloodied. But hey, Lady Macbeth said she'd do whatever it took.

The doorbell rings and I go to open it. Sid's holding a grocery bag full of books and worksheets. "Hey." He lifts the bag. "Guidance wrapped it up like this." He thrusts the package to me. Bumps his toe along the porch. "So how you feeling?" He talks to his foot.

The bag crinkles in my hands. "All right. Still a little tired."

He bumps his toe and then looks up. "I'm sorry, man."

"Yeah, thanks."

We stand for another second. "Ed, let Sid come in. It's cold out there!"

Sid steps in.

"Can I get you something to drink? To eat?" my mom yells from the kitchen.

My body tenses. *Say no. Say no.*

"No, I'm good. Thanks."

The books are now a monstrous weight. I'm unsettled and feeling frantic. "Let's go to my room." We head down the hall. I plop my books next to my syringes. Sid shuts the door. Sits on my bed. He takes in the room. Sees my Biohazard container.

"What the hell is that?" He goes to touch it.

"Don't!" He looks at me. His eyes are wide. "That's where my needles go."

His hand recoils. As if hiding from an animal. "Needles?"

"Yeah." I shrug. "I have to take shots. A few times a day."

"Jesus Christ!" Sid sits up on my bed. He looks around the room as if the needles are lying in wait for him. I'm sweating. He tucks his elbows into his waist. "So what's it you got, exactly?"

"It's called… uh… diabetes."

Sid stares.

"Yeah. Basically my pancreas doesn't work."

Sid continues to stare.

How the hell can I make this clear? A number of thoughts run through my head. None any good. Except, *Google. That's it.*

I sit down at my desk and hop online. I type "define: type one diabetes." The link to Wikipedia pops up. I click it. My neck goes hot.

Way too technical. Too textbook. *Images.* I repeat the search. Same result. I stare for a moment at the useless thumbnails before closing out. I turn to Sid. "I can explain." I clear my throat. "My pancreas doesn't work. I have to take shots to make up for that…"

I ramble on for another five minutes, giving Sid the best explanation I can. I'm no Doc Stevens. Sid alternates between looking at the floor and over my shoulder. I'm light-headed. My mouth is dry.

"Is it contagious?"

"No, it's not," I say. A bit too forcefully.

Sid squints. "So how'd *you* get it?"

I lean on my desk. "I don't know. Just happened."

"Really?" He leans back. "So, could it *just happen* to anybody? To me?"

"Uh… yeah."

It's quiet for a moment. Sid twists his face. Wrinkles his forehead. "Well, not much you can do about that, is there?"

I shake my head. *That's the friggin' truth!*

"Hey, let me tell you about Stacy."

Thank God that's over! I mean… hold up! Who?

"She started giving me eyes in Pilsner's. Then she sat with me at lunch." Sid smiles so wide I hurt. "I mean, you weren't there. She truly wanted to know what was up with you."

Bullshit! "Really?"

"Yeah. And then she showed me her belly button piercing again. Then told me about this party she's having this weekend and how I should come."

I stare at him. The words don't match the sound. It's as if I'm seated across from Ashley or Brittany. *What the hell is this? Stacy? Come on! I'm out one day and… Or has he been planning this all along?* I wrack my brain for something to say. A knock comes at the door. My mom pokes her head in. "You boys doing all right?"

We both say, "Yeah." Mine has no perk to it.

"Ed, why don't you test, so we know where you are before dinner.

Especially after your low."

"All right." It's like she just reminded me to put my underwear *inside* my pants.

"Good. Tell me when you're finished."

"Okay." I tack a bit of snotiness on the "kay."

My mom eyes me narrowly, but leaves. I walk to my nightstand. Grab my kit. Plop it on the bed. Sid turns. "Is that your test thing?"

"Yeah." I go through the motions. Prick my finger. Squeeze for the blood. Sid turns away. I bend over and get the blood on the strip. Sid frowns. My meter beeps: 225. "Damn." I gather the strip to throw it away. Sid's staring at me. "What?"

"Nothin'."

I stop walking to my garbage. "No, really, what's up?" My chest is tight and my temples throb.

"Just the blood, man. It's gross." He turns after he answers.

"Yeah, but I don't really have a choice."

Sid looks up but says nothing. I turn and throw the strip and alcohol pad away. I don't write my reading in my logbook. Instead I open my door and yell down the hall. "Two twenty five, mom!"

Pots and pans clang. "All right. I'll get your insulin."

I hover. Just shift my weight back and forth until she appears. She hands the vial to me. Then tries to kiss my forehead. I pull away. "You okay?"

"Yeah, just fine. Sid's getting me caught up."

She smiles. "Good. Take your shot. Then finish getting caught up."

I close my door. Sid's standing in the middle of the room. I walk past him and grab a syringe. An alcohol pad. My coverage chart. I draw up three units. Sit down on the corner of my desk. Sid paces. I pull up my shirt.

I take the shot. It's so bad that I have to swallow a scream. *How can such small needles hurt so damn much?* I wipe down the wound and discard the needle in the Biohazard container. The "thunk" sounds like a bank-shot. I spin on my heel. "He scores!" Sid's not playing along. He just stands there. His hands are jammed in his pockets. "What's up?" My injection site pulsates. Like some enormous zit.

Sid takes a step. He shrugs. "The needle. How often do you do that?"

He obviously wasn't listening. "Depends. At least three times a day."

His eyes widen. "Are you, uh, are you going to do that at school?"

"Have to."

"Yeah, right." He forces a laugh. Leans into me. "But are you going to do that, like, in front of everybody?"

You mean in front of Stacy? I shake my head. "Probably not. I have to go see Mrs. Lee tomorrow. I bet she'll have me do it down there."

Sid rocks back on his heels. He looks up at the ceiling. "Right, right. So you won't be doing that at the lunch table or anything?"

I have an urge to punch him. *Don't worry, my needles won't interrupt your chance at scoring.* "I doubt it. Why?"

"No reason, no reason." He's still looking at the ceiling. He shuffles his feet and shifts his shoulders. "I mean, if you had somewhere private to go."

"Right. Privacy."

"Yeah." Sid meets my eyes. He immediately looks away.

I don't know what to say. The silence between us howls through my room.

Sid rubs a finger under his nose, snorts, and then looks at the clock. "I'd better get goin'."

I move out of his way.

"I'll get your stuff again, tomorrow."

"All right."

Sid walks to my door. He pauses before going through. Like he might turn and say something. He doesn't. He says goodbye to my mom. The door closes behind him. The thud of it reverberates through my empty bedroom.

My dad lumbers through the back door. Heads straight to the basement. He's got a nice treadmill, squat rack and bench down there.

He's been into all that since he was my age. Reminds me of what Doc Stevens said. *Not right now. Not yet.* I lie back on my bed and rehash my encounter with Sid.

My door opens. "Have you seen your father?"

I sit up. "Isn't he downstairs?"

"I thought he was done and came up."

We both listen. Weights clang. He grunts. "Nope. Still down there."

My mom frowns. "Dinner's ready. You hungry?"

"Sure."

"Everything all right?"

My dad screams downstairs. *I should ask you the same thing.* "Yeah. Just tired."

She nods. "Come on out in a minute."

I step into the hall. He's at the top of stairs. Stopped dead in his tracks. My mom's just said something. Her lip's curled. He looks at her. Then over at me. Like Sid, he pauses for a second before moving. Looking as if he's going to speak. Just like Sid he keeps going without saying a word.

Uncomfortable silence is tonight's entrée. Utensils scrape. My dad sweats. My mom stares into space. I eat and keep track of my carbs. *I guess this is my life now?*

❧

I can't concentrate on these math problems. I'm heavy and thick. I've got some serious leg cramps. I reach across the desk and grab my kit. I plop the blood on and wait: 324. "What?" My cheeks flush. I grab a syringe and an alcohol pad. I step into the hall.

My parents' door is closed. I knock. "Yeah?" I pop my head in. My mom's on the bed, flipping through a magazine.

"I just tested."

She puts her magazine on her lap. "How are you?"

"Three twenty-four." She frowns. I hold up my syringe. "I checked the chart already."

My mom sighs. Ed, you've caught on fast." Her eyes glisten. "I'm sorry. Your father and I..." She shakes her head. Swallows. "You sure

50

you don't need any help?"

"No, I'm all right."

"It'll be okay. I promise."

I leave their room and turn the corner toward the kitchen. My dad's standing at the sink. His back to me. But the light casts his reflection in the window. I can see his eyes. He's looking right at me.

I stutter-step. "Hey, Dad."

He finishes the beer in his hand and sets the empty bottle in the sink. I go to the fridge. "Grab me another."

I get my insulin and his beer. Close the door. I hand him his beverage. He's facing me. Leaning on the counter. "Thanks." I cross the room and sit at the table. His eyes are on me. That weird vibe builds on my neck. I look up. Sure enough, he's staring. He immediately turns away. I return to my injection. It's there again. I draw up my insulin. *Just say something or stop staring.* He does neither.

I bite my lip so that I don't squeal when the needle pushes through. I take my shot. I've got an anthill-like mound from my other injection. I think now I'll have a matching set. I deposit the syringe and return my insulin.

"How's it going?" His voice slides and dips over the beer.

"All right." I look down at the worn out linoleum.

"Yeah? Really?"

Is he buzzed or being sensitive? "Yeah."

"Good, good." He passes a hand from the back to the front of his head. He smiles. "I have to tell you, I've been freakin' out with all this." He laughs. It's an uncomfortable sound.

I'm both embarrassed and angry. But I don't know where either emotion should be directed. I shuffle my feet. "It's all right. I understand."

He sets his beer down. He steps toward me. All of his movements appear measured. "You do?"

I nod. *How does he not get this?* "Uncle Brian."

He looks away. His chin quivers. But he holds it together. Lets out a long sigh. "It's just all flooding back… and I can't… I don't…" He puts a hand on my shoulder. I tense up. "I don't know what to do."

The weight of his hand is overwhelming. The stench of his beer equal to it. "Neither do I, but mom does. She always seems to."

He eyes me for a moment. Then we stand for a while in silence. I'm so tired it's like I've been in the ocean fighting waves all day. My body is still rocking to their motion. He squeezes my shoulder again. "Life's a crapshoot."

Chapter 7

And when we have our naked frailties hid,
That suffer in exposure, let us meet
And question this most bloody piece of work
To know it further. (2.3.148-151)

IT'S WEIRD BEING IN SCHOOL AND NOT IN CLASSES. It's a lot like being at the zoo. We're passing class after class of kids bent to desks, writing. Or slouched low in their seats, trying to stay awake. I stop at Pilsner's room and listen. "'Macbeth does murder sleep!" My mom continues on. I stay and listen. "Glamis hath murder'd sleep, and therefore Cawdor shall sleep no more, Macbeth shall sleep no more!" Mr. P stops there and asks a question. I strain to hear if anybody answers.

"Ed!" My mom's at the corner. Waving to me. I listen for one more moment. Then join up with her.

We turn the corner and come to Mrs. Lee's office. It's across the hall from the gym. The clack of hockey sticks on floorboards fills the air. I peer through the windows. It's my class but I don't see Sid. I do see Mr. Miner chewing his whistle like a cow does cud. I bolt when he looks over.

"Mrs. Devlin. Ed." Mrs. Lee stands at her desk. "Come in," She gestures like a flight attendant. My mom and I park ourselves in the neon-colored, vinyl chairs that flank the room. "You're looking better, Ed."

"Thanks." I know she's lying. I took a good look at myself in the mirror after I showered this morning. Not much has changed.

53

Mrs. Lee turns to my mom. "How's the transition going?"

My mom sighs. "As I expected. I bet it'll be a solid two weeks before we can get a regular pattern." She pauses. "Right now, all over the place."

Mrs. Lee's eyes widen. She looks like an owl. "What about hypoglycemia?" My mom chuckles. Then she takes out my logbook. "Where do I begin?"

I just love it when adults talk about me as if I'm not sitting smack-dab in the room with them. My second grade teacher always did that. She and the other teacher would just blab away in the hall. About all of us. Regardless of the fact that we were right there. Milling about and eating glue.

I tune out of the conversation to stare out the window at the cold grey sky. It's placid and these chairs are comfy.

Loud squeaking footsteps shuffle over the linoleum. They snap me back to my senses. Mark's stumbling through the door. Holding his nose. Sid's right behind him.

"Uh...Mark got hurt." Sid looks over Mark's shoulder. His eyes bounce inside his head.

"Have him sit here." Mrs. Lee indicates a seat adjacent to us. A trickle of blood runs from between Mark's fingers to a stain on his T-shirt. He sits with a thud. But doesn't speak. Mrs. Lee attends to him. Sid steps back. He gives me a head nod. But says nothing. I nod back. He turns from me and pays real close attention to what Mrs. Lee is doing.

"It might be broken." Mrs. Lee frowns. My mom peeks and nods. Mark's nose is angled toward his cheek. "What happened?" Mark doesn't speak. Doesn't even shrug. Sid answers.

"We were playing floor hockey and Mark got checked into the wall."

Mrs. Lee gives Mark a towel to clean up his hands. She puts a bag of ice onto his nose. His eyes are closed. His body is rigid. "Thank you, Sid. You can go back to P.E. now."

Sid hovers for a second. Looks from Mrs. Lee to me. His eyes narrow. He holds the look. Like he's trying to tell me something using telepathy. I squint and lean forward. "What?" Sid cocks an eyebrow and then returns to class.

"Yes, it's broken." Mrs. Lee adjusts the phone. Mark's right leg is pumping. "Okay. See you then." She hangs up. "Mark, your mother will be here soon. How about I move you somewhere more comfortable?" She escorts him to the same cot I used.

"Never a dull moment." Mrs. Lee sits back down with us.

"You've got a mini E.R. down here. Complete with all the drama." The two nurses smile. I look back out the window.

"So where were we?" Mrs. Lee asks.

"I think we're all set. Except for lunchtime protocol."

"He has to test and inject with me."

"Then he can eat his lunch in the cafeteria?"

"Absolutely." Mrs. Lee turns to me. "You can inject first. Save yourself a trip back, after lunch. Sound all right?"

"Sure." I catch Mark's silhouette behind the sheet. He's pressing on his forehead. *What the hell happened?* I know Sid. Something's not right. I turn. Mrs. Lee and my mom are looking at me expectantly. I do what I normally do in class when I'm not paying attention. I pull something out of my butt. "Great, great, sounds great to me."

I've spent a good chunk of the afternoon doing homework. Math and science. I finished Act II of *Macbeth*. The noblemen really could have used *CSI*. Macbeth gets away with the murder. Everybody believes the sons paid someone to do it. They did run away after the murder, so it makes sense. Macbeth becomes king because they did. I guess it was his fate after all.

It's 4:30 and Sid still hasn't dropped by. I go to the door. Maybe he's lying on the stoop because someone mugged him for my books. Or maybe he's just climbing up my steps. Panting and out of breath. He missed the bus and ran all the way to my house.

My door has one of those little oval windows. It's difficult to see through because it's frosted and has flower-like patterns cut into the glass. But I can get a good look if I tilt my head at just the right angle. My books are piled on the little decorative bench on the front porch. Some papers try desperately to fly free in the wind. No Sid.

I step out and almost trip over the lip of the door. I steady myself on my books. They're just the remnants from my locker and some stupid worksheets. I raise a hand to my eyes. Look down the driveway. In case Sid's just departing. Nothing. Just cracked macadam and oil stains.

I carry my books inside. I want to fling them across the room. But my mom appears. "Hey, more homework?"

"Yeah." I let the books dangle.

She puts a hand on her hip. "Why didn't you ask Sid in?"

I would have if I'd seen him "He... uh... had to run. His mom needed to bring him to the dentist or something."

My mom looks me over. I examine the arm of the couch. "Well, you might as well go work on that."

Or I could jam a pen into my eyeball. Scoop it out and turn it into a lollipop. "All right." I tuck my books under my arm and go to my bedroom.

I sit at my desk and stare at my work. I have no interest in doing any of it. A mental image of my logbook keeps invading. I haven't had any more lows but my levels haven't been exactly normal either. I've been bouncing around 240 and 300. My mom smiles like it's okay. I know it's not. I know it will take time and all... but now... this nonsense with Sid. *What the hell? I need this?*

I test: 179. "I'll give it a B." I stare at the blood on my finger for a second before wiping it off. I've got these weird flecks underneath. Like freckles. They're embedded within the whorl of my fingerprints. But they're not freckles. They're scabs.

I go to the kitchen. My mom's got another concoction baking in the oven. I flip the light on and stare at it through the window. It's some casserole thing. I go to the garage. My mom's working on a project. She jumps at the sound of the door.

"Jesus! You scared me."

I consider using my little joke, but don't. "Sorry."

"Is everything all right? Are you low?"

Christ, my name's not Diabetes. "No, just hungry." I look behind her. At the collection of fabric. She sees me looking and glances at the sketches next to her. "What are you making?" She looks at the fabric as if it's a surprise to her. Like somebody else hauled it in here without her knowledge. *Why do people do this? It's so fake.*

"This? Oh, just a little something I thought of." She looks at me. "It's for your dad. For Christmas. But it's a surprise, okay?"

"Sure." I nod. "How long until dinner?"

"Is your father home?"

I shrug. She steps to the garage windows and peers out. Looks for his truck. "Yup." She makes the listening face. "Still downstairs."

Shocker!

"Probably another hour." She returns to her work.

I hover for a second longer. To watch her cut fabric. I want to ask her about Sid. Get some advice. But she may not be the best person to ask. I slip out of the garage and go back to my room.

❧

My meter beeps: 55. My mom pours a tall glass of juice. I drink.

"How much insulin did you take?"

I grab my logbook. But I haven't filled it in for today. I grab a pen. She sees.

"You didn't write it in?"

I shake my head.

"Can you remember how many carbs you ate?"

"Sixty."

"And what's your ratio?"

"Fifteen to one."

"Right. So how much did you take?"

The number emerges in spite of the still-fuzziness of the low. "I took six units."

She sighs and folds her arms across her chest. "You've got to write everything down. That way you'll remember."

57

I stare at the floor.

Her chair scrapes. "Test in another twenty minutes. I'll be in the garage."

I wait until she's gone and then move to the couch. I fall into it. Turn the TV on. *Jeopardy* appears. I watch and can't formulate a single question.

My dad walks in. I've heard the expression, *If looks could kill then he'd be dead.* Well, if looks could transform you, I'd be a pile of shit. He's still damp from his workout. I'm sprawled out on the couch as energetic as mold. He looks at the TV. Sneers. Tracks down the remote like a hunter a deer. "You can watch what you want. This is almost over."

He throws a dismissive wave. Starts to walk away.

"Really, it's fine. I have to do my homework anyway." I grab the remote. Sit up.

He stops. Looks at me. "You sure?"

I thrust the remote toward him. But he sits down in the recliner. Props his feet up and opens up his hands like he's about to receive a pass. He's so fluid. He makes it look as if we've done this every day of my life. I shatter this notion when I toss the remote wide. It skips across the floor. He lowers the leg-rest. Snatches the remote from just under the lip of the love seat. Settles back in. I hate him for all the genes he didn't pass along to me. Seriously. I'm not sure I could be any less like him. *Maybe I should get a paternity test?*

I squish down into the couch. I can get up at the first commercial of whatever god-awful sports recap event he turns on. The final Jeopardy category comes back on the screen. Even my dad can't resist that blue and white challenge. Alex informs us, "Again, our topic is Sports Stars."

My dad sits up. "Now that's my kind of category."

The screen zooms in: *This cyclist survived Testicular and Lung cancer, and is now the premier athlete of his sport.* The question is so obvious I almost yell out, "Who is Lance Armstrong?" My dad pulls into himself. The question isn't the problem. He knows it's Lance. It's the memory. My dad sat and read Lance's book, *It's Not About the Bike*, to Brian as he lay dying in the hospital. My mom said the book was for inspiration. I read it once my dad no longer needed it. After, I knew what my mom meant. But seeing my dad now, I'm not so certain. He's as pale as smoke. Sitting rigid in his chair. Paralyzed by a question from a game show.

Chapter 8

Thou hast it now...all
As the Weird Women promised, and I fear
Thou play'd'st most foully for't. Yet it was said
It should not stand in thy posterity. (3.1.1-4)

"Ed. Ed! Jesus Christ! Ed!"

I open my eyes. One burns against the carpet so I close it. Above me, my dad is yelling.

"Kathy! Ka————thy!"

Footsteps pound in the hall. I'm on my floor. The room is sliding away from me. Hands are on my head and back. I'm being rolled.

"Ed, hold on. You're okay." My mom squats in front of me. "You're having a low." Her mouth isn't in sync with the words. I try to answer. Nothing comes. I slump forward. My dad pulls me back. My mom leaves and the room whirls violently. Like a carousel.

I try focusing on something—the light switch, the corner of my desk—but I feel nauseous. I close my eyes. For a moment I'm fine. Almost peaceful. But something ignites inside. My right arm twitches. Just bounces in the air. My head jerks. I open my eyes and loud static—like "snow" on the TV—fills my head. I try to stand. My dad keeps me in place. "Hey, relax." I snap away with a shoulder shrug. I have to get out of here.

I crawl toward the door. A hand grabs me. I turn and shove. *Off me!*

My dad rocks back. I'm on my feet in a second. The static is crackling off the walls.

It's like I'm dreaming one of those dreams where I know I'm dreaming but can't do anything to stop. My dad stands. His eyes are hooded by his eyebrows. I'm hunched. Arms dangling. Cocked at my sides. My breath is raspy. My heart hammers. *Hit him! Do it!* I take a step forward. My dad does the same.

My head cracks the wall with one shot. My arms follow with one-two punches below where my head went through. The static is at an eardrum-splitting decibel. The powder of broken drywall fills my nostrils. Crumbs bunch between my toes. The sensation makes me want to rip off my skin. My dad steps in front of me. He speaks. The sound is meaningless. I lunge and catch him with a wide, arching punch to the jaw. The shock stings through my arm and rattles my teeth. The static breaks another degree. I taste blood.

My dad stumbles back and onto the bed. My legs are taken out. My head smacks the carpet and bounces. The static stops. A hand rips down my shorts and delivers the white-hot sensation of an injection. I scream. Carpet brushes against my tongue. I stop fighting.

I'm still as ice. My breathing has changed from spasmodic rasps to a soft hush. My heart has regained its normal cadence. I roll over. My dad is on my bed. Holding his jaw. Staring wide-eyed. My mom sits on the floor at his feet. She's holding a thick syringe. A drop of milky fluid glistens at its tip. Definitely not insulin. My meter lies on the floor next to her. They both stare at me. Fragments of my wall line the space between us. I trace the fallout to three gaping holes. I rub a hand over my face. Even though part of me already knows the answer—the part that feels shame and self-loathing. The part that believes my dad's right about me—I ask, "What happened?"

ംഗ്ൊ

It's morning and I'm thick and heavy. Like my joints are filled with mortar. My mouth has a toothpaste-like film to it. My head throbs. I stare at my ceiling for a while. Then I sit up. There are holes in my wall.

The night before floods back.

I grab my meter. Hesitate before testing. I've felt this way before. The reading is going to be high. I do the routine and wait the five seconds: HI. That's what the meter displays. Not, "Hi" like, "Hey, how ya' doin'?" No, like "My scale doesn't go that high, moron!" My stomach swirls like it's being flushed. Blood drains from my face. I cup my forehead with my palm and breathe. I test again: HI.

I throw my meter onto the bed and bury my face into my pillow. I don't cry. I scream into the pillow and squeeze it tight. I have to face my mom. The sooner the better. I have an appointment in a few hours. I can't show up like *this*. But last night… *I'm a mess*. It's only 6:00 AM. The day is already shot.

I set my head on the tank and enjoy its cool touch. My screw-up spills from me. I labor down the hall and into my parents' conversation.

"It would be nice if you could be there." My mom leans on her hip while she speaks.

My dad shifts his weight and balances his lunch container and thermos. "I can't. You know that. This is one of the last jobs before the winter. We need the money." He levels his eyes on her when he says this. Like he used to when I was younger. Hell, like he still does.

"Do what you have to." She turns from him and walks to the kitchen. My dad sighs and looks around the house like he's doing inventory. Until he lands on me. He freezes. Watches me for a second. Shakes his head. Turns away.

He leaves. I turn the corner. My mom's talking to herself. She jumps when she sees me. "Jesus, Ed!"

"No, just regular Ed." She doesn't laugh. I hover in place.

"What is it? What's wrong?"

How does she know? "I'm high. Really high."

"How high?"

"The meter just said HI. There wasn't a number."

"Damn." Her eyes bug. "Well, grab your insulin." She plants her hands on her hips. "After last night I should have expected this. Probably should have woken you up at three. But I was just so tired."

I grab my supplies and coverage chart. There's no box for "Off the chart." I turn to her. "How much?"

She looks at me. The chart. The insulin. She closes her eyes. "Fifteen. Yeah, that should work."

I nod and go to it.

She sits down next to me. She's beyond haggard. "You okay?" She rubs my cheek.

I lean on the table. "Yeah."

"Last night." She pauses. "That was scary, wasn't it?" She pats my hand.

"I was low. Right?"

She nods and her lips draw a tight line. "It's different when you are asleep."

"So if Dad hadn't heard me… and you hadn't given me that shot…" I can't find the words.

"Yes, you could have been in serious trouble. At minimum, you'd be back in the hospital." She strokes the back of my hand. "If you were low all night, you could be in a coma. And you might not wake up from that."

My head throbs. "Really?"

She nods. "I've seen it a few times. Two years ago we lost a little boy. His parents thought he was just sleeping through his cold. His glucose level was 7. You slip into a coma at 10."

A chill runs up my spine. My heart pounds. "You tested me last night. What was I?"

Her jaw tightens. "Twenty-two."

My head falls to my chest.

"*You* will be fine. We just have to get you straightened out. It takes time." She grabs my chin and pulls it toward her face." Your dad will be fine, too. We'll fix the holes in your wall." She lets go. "But, Ed. *You* have to do your absolute best. Write everything down. I have to go back to work this weekend. That means it's just you and your father."

God, no! I don't know if I can do this. My throat swells. "I will." I tighten my face and try to hold on. It's useless. I lose it and cry on the kitchen table.

⚬⚬⚬

My meter beeps: 320.

"At least you're coming down." My mom frowns at the screen.

I do the same. "I guess so."

"We leave in an hour. We'll see what Doc Stevens says."

I go to my room and dig out *Macbeth*. I find Act Three, scene one. Maybe it will take my mind off the visit.

Macbeth's going to have his right-hand man, Banquo, whacked. What an ass! Macbeth's having him killed because he doesn't wantthe prophecies about Banquo to come true: that his kids will be kings and he'll be greater than Macbeth. What a prick. Or maybe it's because Macbeth realizes that Banquo's on to him?

The waiting room is the same as before. Sick little kids and their moms dot the chairs. They sneeze. Sweat. Cry. I look for a seat. My mom checks us in. *Is that Mark?* I do a double take. *Yeah, it is.*

Mark's sitting under a poster of a kitten with a ball of yarn. The message reads, "I'm doing the best I can." He's got his head tilted back against the wall. His eyes are shut. His nose is crooked. Bent. Sliding off his face. Deformed. He's got bruises under his eyes and around the bridge of his sloppy nose. I'm staring like some psychopath. He opens his eyes. "Ed? What's up?"

I walk over and sit next to him. "Hey, how's your nose?" I know it's abrupt. Like meeting someone with a handicap—say one arm or deafness—and instead of making small talk, launching into questions about his ailment: *So how do you get dressed? Do you have a special shower? Can you hear anything? No, I don't sign? Oh, I know what that means.* I just can't help it.

Mark touches his nose. "It's all right. They're going to reset it."

I touch my own nose. "How do they do that?"

"They put these metal spike things—like knife sharpeners—up your nostrils. Then bang them and move your nose back into place."

The words "bang them" in reference to metal spikes up your nose should never be spoken. This sounds like absolute torture. But Mark's smiling like he's holding the winning Lotto ticket. He looks at me for a second. Averts his eyes. Then asks, "You here for your… uh… die… uh…"

"Betes."

"Yeah, that." His ears redden.

I don't say anything else. My mom's talking to the receptionist and another woman who is standing at the counter. I turn back to Mark. His profile flips my stomach. From the angle I'm at it looks as if he has no nose. Just a continuous curve of cheek and lip. He turns back to me. The view is a little better. Not much. I have to ask. "What the hell happened?"

Mark gives me a cold look. Something swims just under the surface. "You're friend, Sid. He's got some problems."

It's like someone's sucker-punched me. *Who are you?* I give it a second. "I hear you."

Mark crinkles his forehead. Screws his eyes onto me.

I go to speak. To tell him about Sid. But don't get the chance. We're interrupted by the click-clack of high heels.

"Markus?"

Mark's—or should I say Markus's—eyes roll in his head. I look up. There's a hot chick standing there. Like blue-flame-a-day-in-hell hot. She's got to be almost six feet tall. Long, chestnut hair. So wavy she looks like one of those girls on the hair dye bottles my mom buys. Not a wrinkle. Not a blemish. I swear, there are miniature lights, softly glowing under her skin. She leans over to speak to Mark. I swear I try not to stare. But am unsuccessful.

"Who's this?" She flashes me a restaurant hostess's smile.

"This is Ed. He's in my class. Ed, my mom." Mark pauses for a second. "He's, uh… he's got diabetes."

My happy thoughts fizzle. I was picturing Mark's mom and me on some deserted island. She was wearing this bikini made out of palm leaves. All of a sudden a gust of sea breeze came along, and POP! Now, I'm back to reality. Mark's mom's face is turned downward. She gives me the sad puppy-dog eyes. Extends her hand. I shake it. There's some redemption. Her skin is like touching a sun-kissed blanket.

"Nice to meet you," she says. I mumble the same. She turns from me and looks at Mark with an I-need-to-talk-to-you look. I pretend to be interested in the magazine on the seat next to me. *I never knew there were so many fun decorations that could be made with a hatbox.*

Mark stands and gathers up his coat. His mom waits. It's as if she's at a photo shoot. "Hey, I never finished telling you about Sid and my nose."

"No, you didn't."

"You, uh… you wanna come over tonight? It's not like I'll be doing anything."

I almost say, "No, I've got to see what Sid's up to." The response is so automatic that trying to stop it causes me to sputter like I'm having a seizure. I regain my composure. "Sure. You want me to call you later? Make sure that you're all right?"

Mark laughs. "Yeah, sure. I'll be fine though. This isn't the first bone I've busted."

I cock an eyebrow. "All right. I'll call you later."

Mark's mom turns and smiles before she walks away.

Hey, I'll see YOU, later. Mother and son disappear around the corner.

My mom crosses to me. "Let's go."

We claim an exam room and sit. Doc Stevens busts right in. He takes my logbook. "Hmmmmm… Hmmmmph… Hmmmmm," He flips through my pages. He's got one hand on his chin. He's examining my results like he's staring at a crossword puzzle. The way he keeps shifting, I wonder if his ass is all right. With a final, "Hmmmmph," he sets the book down on his knee. "How are you feeling?"

Like a fish that's been hooked and thrown back. "All right."

Doc leans forward like he needs more of my words to brace him from falling.

I look at my mom. So does Doc. "Not bad. Better than I did on Monday. But last night was tough."

"What about last night?"

My mom blushes to crimson. She sits upright, shakes her head and clears her throat. "I had to give him glucogon."

Doc leans back. Sneaks a look at me. "Really?"

My mom nods. "He was out of control. About to pass out. Twenty-two."

Doc frowns. "How have your levels been today?" He picks the logbook back up. "I don't see any here."

My mom glares at me. I turn away. "I, uh… didn't write them in. Yet."

"Okay. Tell me this morning's."

I clear my throat. "I was high."

"Ed, an actual number. Please."

"That's what the meter read. HI. No number."

Doc scribbles on the pad across his lap. "Do you understand what that means?"

I shrug.

"Your meter can measure to 600. If it reads HI, you were over that."

It's pin-drop quiet. I shift my weight on the bed. The paper crinkles.

"I'm not trying to scare you. You just need to know this." Doc flips back the logbook pages. "Looks like you have been doing fine until after dinner. Then you bottom out."

I *was* utterly exhausted when I went to bed last night. My skin might have been clammy. I just can't remember.

Doc shoots me a sympathetic look. Like he's reading my thoughts. "Ed, hey. It will be all right. This takes time to get used to. Months even." He nods. "I know that's frustrating. One day at a time. You know?"

I nod, but I'm not sure I believe that everything will be all right.

"Let's make some adjustments here." Doc writes on a Post-It note that he's stuck to the back of my logbook. "Twenty to one ratio for the Humalog. Let's cut the Lantus to sixteen units." He looks up. "All right?"

"Yeah. Okay."

"Excellent. Now keep up the good work. I want to see you in a month. Just before Christmas." He smiles. "Put a bow on your logbook."

More like a noose. "I will."

I walk to the end of the hall. Doc and my mom stay behind. They talk. I check out the fish tank. There's a little kid wiping his boogers on the side. The fish are trying to eat them through the glass.

My mom joins me and we head to the car.

"Can I go to Mark's house tonight?"

She opens her mouth but doesn't speak. She makes a left turn and then looks at me. "He's that same boy from Mrs. Lee's office?"

"Yeah. He was there today. Didn't you see him?"

"No. Sorry. Missed him."

"His nose is broken. He has to get it reset."

"Looked that way when I saw it." She purses her lips. "How well do you know Mark?"

"I don't know. He's in my classes."

"So you and Sid are going to his house?"

Hell no! "Uh, no. I mean, Sid's going to call and let me know what he's up to."

My mom checks her mirrors. "All right, but…" She doesn't finish her sentence. She stops at a red light.

"But what?"

She sighs. "I need to speak with Mark's mom first."

"Why?"

She rolls her eyes. I was in fourth grade when she first tortured me with this. I went to a sleepover party at this kid Jeff's. After his parents went to bed he started ragging on me about how my mom had called to tell his mom that I was afraid of the dark. The other kids laughed. I, of course, called Jeff a liar. He made me prove it by spending an hour in his basement with the lights off. He had a scarier-than-hell-perfect-for-a-murder-scene-dirt-basement. Jeff opened the door after an hour. I don't know which I was happiest about. Making it the full sixty minutes. Or that no one noticed my wet pajamas.

"Do you remember last night? You're lucky I'm even considering it."

My ears burn. Even though I know what Doc said. Even though I know she's just looking out for me. I don't want her to have to make this phone call. Just like I don't want this crap between Sid and me. The crap between her and my father. The bucket of crap that comes with diabetes. I just want a normal life. Sid back. My parents happy.

The light turns green. She drives. We don't speak.

Chapter 9

Thou marvel'st at my words, but hold thee still.
Things bad begun make strong themselves by ill. (3.2.61-62)

THERE'S THIS GUY. One of those crazy, outdoor adventure, I-live-at-Eastern-Mountain-Sports types. Well, he's out hiking by himself. Through these narrow passages in the desert. Lo and behold he gets stuck. Not stuck like he needs some Crisco and he can wiggle loose. No, he's stuck permanently. Because a rock the size of a small car rolled from its perch within this canyon—where it had sat for thousands of years—in some weird cosmic coincidence and pinned this guy's right arm. But that's not the end of the story. Far from it.

This guy had nerves of steel. Because after he's been pinned for a few days and realizes there's no way out, what does he do? He cuts off his arm. Just takes out a regular pocketknife and saws away until he's free. Unbelievable. But at the same time exactly how I feel. I'd cut off a piece of my body right now just to get out of my house. Of course with this disease I might lose a limb without even trying.

My mom called Mark's house after I looked it up for her. There was no answer. "They're probably still at the hospital." I went to my room.

That's when I read about that guy. Mr. Pilsner sent the article home for us to read. For some comparison essay assignment with *Macbeth*. I'm right on point with the class, having read through Act Three, scene three. Macbeth's hired thugs killed Banquo. That was gory and all. But I'm not really sure what a hit-job has to do with hiking and hacking off body parts.

Anyway, now I'm willing my bedroom wall to fall on me. If I have to sit around here one more damn night... The phone rings.

"Ed. Phone."

I tear out of my room and my mom hands me the phone. She's got that furrowed brow-who-is-it? look. I ignore her and cradle the phone to my ear. "Hello?"

"Ed, it's Mark. What's up?"

"Hey, how's your nose." My mom mouths, "Is that Mark?" I turn away. *Who the hell else would it be?*

"Hurts a little. Not bad. I got a stupid splint going across it, though."

I remember seeing some NBA player wearing one of those and asking my dad about it. "He's a man. Broken nose. Still playing." He then looked at me like he wanted to snap me in two and turn me into a splint.

Mark continues. "Did you still want to come over? My mom won't let me go out. But you can still come here if you want."

"All right." I turn around. My mom's still standing there like a gargoyle. "Hold on..." I put the phone to my chest.

"I have to speak with his mother first."

I try to stare her down. But she holds on without even a flicker of a twitch. "Mark? Um... my mom wants to talk to your mom."

"Uh... okay... hold on." He calls for her. I glare at my mom again. Trying to impress upon her that I don't want her to act like an idiot. She yanks the phone from my hand.

"Hello? Yes, Mrs. Hughes? This is Kathy Devlin..."

She goes on for a solid ten minutes. She yaks away about me and diabetes. Mark and his nose. She even gives Mark's mom advice on how to control the swelling. What to do if his nose really gushes. "You can always use a tampon."

❧

My reflection is still awful. My cowlick pushes the hair on the back of my head all about like a crop circle. I lean toward my mirror. My books tumble to the floor and vomit their worksheets.

I gather them. Put them in a pile. Reach for the door. My heel crinkles below me. There's a paper on the floor covered in loopy green ink. I pick it up and inhale the stench of perfume and cigarettes. I read:

Sid sweetie,

What's up? You seem so lonely these past few days. Do you need some TLC? 'Cuz you know I can give it to you. I think it's hot what you did to that Mark kid. All my friends agree. I mean, who the hell does he think he is? No one talks to me that way. You should totally come by my house Friday night. My parents will be out. That is if you wanna come and play. But just make sure you don't bring your sick friend. The one who's out 'cuz of that disease thing. Disgusting. No thank you. 'K?

Stacy

I'm lightheaded. I grab my test kit. An enormous weight rests on my shoulders. Like someone is leaning on me. Watching. I curl the kit close to my body. Shield it with my hands. Like smart kids cover their tests. *That disease thing. Disgusting.* My face flushes. My throat fills up. My meter beeps: 202. I squeeze my eyeballs. It's no use.

I cry and feel stupid. I wipe my tears with my sleeve and steady myself. I take a deep breath.

"You ready, Ed?"

"One second." I stare at the note lying next to me on the bed. I snatch it up and crumble it like I'm actually trying to stuff it through my skin. I stand up and look at my garbage can. Instead, I put it in my pocket.

My mom's in the hall. "All right. Let's go." I move to the car before she can ask me about my puffy face.

She pulls up to Mark's. "Make sure you test again. Make sure you call your father by ten." I scamper out of the car. Mark's mom walks past me.

"Hi, Ed. Mark's inside. Go on in." She smiles. I fall up their patio steps.

Mark's on the couch in the living room amidst a pile of mismatched throw pillows. He's got cotton up his nose. The splint across his face. Feet propped up on a scratched coffee table. I look around: the worn hardwood floors. The walls that need paint. *This is just like my house.*

"Hey." Mark turns. Shoves some pillows aside.

I sit next to him. Something squirms within the couch. He's watching *Jeopardy* and I almost laugh out loud. "What's with the cotton balls?"

"I started bleeding again. My mom stuck these up there. She told me that your mom said tampons would work even better."

I shake my head in disgust.

Mark's mom reappears. I try not to stare. But she's wearing one of those athletic outfits—the kind that women wear to show off their bodies, but never actually work out in. She may or may not work out. But she's working the outfit just fine. Mark watches me eyeballing her rear. He punches my arm.

"Would you boys like anything?"

"Ed might."

I punch his arm. We both laugh.

"I've got diet soda, Ed."

My face flushes. "Um… thanks."

"It's either that or water. She doesn't buy anything else." He shrugs. "It's not so bad."

I turn away from the TV. There's artwork everywhere. The house is filled with "pieces." There's a twisted metal flower on Mark's dining room table. These crazy wooden sculptures that look like they fell out of my history textbook are in each of the corners. Paintings with ridiculously vivid, acid-trip colors hang on the walls. These aren't prints but the real deal. Oil on canvas.

We don't have one sculpture or abstract work at my house. Just crappy pictures in plastic frames. Knickknacks from the dollar store. Mark's got the standard family pictures on the mantel. But of course they aren't standard. They're black and white. Candid shots. Mark's mom is hiding from the camera. Mark's smiling so wide the picture almost needs a bigger frame. I'm jealous. "Is your family really into art?"

He turns. Sees what I'm looking at. "Just my mom and aunt. My aunt took those pictures last year."

I sweep my arm across the room. "What about the rest?"

Mark sits up. "My mom does the metal-work and sculpting."

"The paintings?"

Mark lowers back to the couch. His ears redden. "I painted those. But my sketches are better."

I look from him to the painting closest to me. It's fan-freaking-tastic. Like something Monet or one of those other famous guys would do.

Mark gets up. I follow him down the hall. His room is like walking into an artist's head. His walls are covered in sketches. He's got these amazing pictures from the baseboard to the ceiling. Some are cartoon-like. Giant heads and small feet. Others are life-like. So real they're spooky. I'm speechless. Mark's drawn all the members of our class. All of our teachers, too. I look better in his drawing than I do in real life.

He's got a bookshelf crammed with sketchbooks. Like the ones he always totes around. There's a braided rug on his floor that's designed to look like an open mouth. I stand on the tongue and chuckle.

Mark grabs a sketchbook. "Check this out." He lays it on his desk. I flip through. It's filled with all these scenes from school. One of Mr. P. lecturing. He's got a book in hand. He's tilted. Mouth is wide. Like he's a preacher. A kid is slumped on his desk off in the corner. Drool puddles around his face.

I keep flipping and am stunned. Skills, skills, skills. This kid's got them. I don't have jack. I turn to him. "Your nose."

"What? Is it bleeding?" He puts a hand to it.

"No, I mean, did you draw what happened?"

Mark smiles.

The picture before me is a comic book layout sort of thing. The first frame shows P.E. class. The floor hockey sticks getting passed out. Mr. Miner barrel-chested and yelling. The next is a divided class. Separate teams. Both looking sloppy in wrinkled shorts and shirts. There's a group in the corner by the bleachers. Sid and Stacy and the rest. Mark's drawn Sid's head cocked to the right. Stacy sports her ubiquitous shorts with "Princess" stenciled on the rear.

The next frame is a tight shot down Mark's arm. He's chasing the puck. The trio stands before him. They lean on their sticks. Devoid of any athletic prowess. Sid's in the corner. Making an approach.

Then Mark is on the ground. As is Stacy. Their feet are tangled. Next shot, Mark is on his feet. He extends a hand to Stacy. Her face is twisted. Like something undigested just made its way back up.

Next, Stacy's standing with one hand on her hip. The other is in the air, punctuating her curse. She leans into Mark. He stands with his hands raised in the air. But he's saying something back. His lips are curled. His eyes leveled. Lurking in the corner of the page is Sid's profile, lunging.

I look at Mark. He won't meet my eyes. He just wants me to turn the page. I do and find an explosion. There is nothing but a nose. A wall. An eruption of blood. Mark has carefully detailed the contours of the concrete. The rivulets of his blood running down.

Blank pages follow. Clammy sweat covers my back. I pat the bulge in my pants. Pull out my kit before I realize what I've done. I turn, but Mark looks vacant. Like he's still seeing that moment. I fumble with my kit. Get the blood on the strip and wait: 175. I clean everything up. I hold my alcohol pad and used test strip. Mark points to his garbage can. It looks like a rock. I cross the room. He speaks.

"You need anything?"

I watch my waste fall. "No I'm good. So, what did you say?"

Mark smiles an evil little grin. "To Stacy?"

I cross the room. "Yeah."

"She stands up all hot and bothered and starts yelling. I didn't listen to most of it. But I did hear her when she did that stupid air-quote thing."

Stacy does this all the time. Really, it is stupid. I bet the only reason she doesn't get made fun of is because she's hot. Guys worship her. Girls are petrified not to be associated with her.

"She said, 'You watch yourself, ass! These here are some *precious goods!*'" Mark runs a hand through his hair. "I just couldn't resist. I said, 'Any goods you have, aren't precious anymore.'"

I laugh out loud. So does Mark.

"She starts asking me who the hell I think I am. I'm waiting for Mr. Martin to blow the whistle. So I just throw up my hands and toss her a look."

"You didn't even see him. Did you?"

Mark shakes his head. We're both quiet for a moment. "After, Mr. Martin asked Sid to walk me to Mrs. Lee's. While we're in the hall he says, 'Watch your mouth, or you'll get worse.'"

There's no way that Mark's lying. I've heard Sid's dad use that exact same sentence. My hand brushes over my leg. The letter hidden in my pocket crumples. I pull it out. "I… uh… you should read this." I pass it to him. He reads.

Mark exhales. "Whoa. She's a piece of work." He looks at me. "I'm sorry man, that's raw. Even if he is your friend…"

"I know." *Is he still my friend?* I picture Sid for a second. Just a brief image of him and me years ago. When we were little. We were running around the yard playing. My dad had just gotten back from a fishing trip with my Uncle Brian. It was so normal, then. Now, it's totally messed up. I know there isn't a way to get it back. Not like it was before.

Mark sits at his desk. He starts to say something but then shakes his head. He pauses and flashes another grin. Makes me think the screws in his head aren't just loose. They've come completely undone. Are clanging around inside his skull. "Don't worry, he'll get his." He laughs. "Maybe he already is."

"What do you mean?"

"He's with Stacy now."

I shuffle a foot across his carpet. "He is?"

Mark lifts an eyebrow. "Yeah. You didn't know?"

"I guessed, but…" I don't finish. I don't know what to say.

Mark stands. "To hell with him!" He looks down. "Oh, damn." His nose is bleeding.

"Time for those tampons." We laugh and he bleeds.

'Mom!" Mark heads to the bathroom. His mother comes down the hall and joins him.

"Shit! All right. Sit down."

This is probably a good time to call my dad. I push the buttons and wait. He answers on the third ring. "Hello." This sounds like an effort.

"Hey, it's me. You want to come pick me up?" No response. There's a hum of silence. Like the fluorescent bulbs in Doc's office.

He grunts. "You at that kid, Mark's?"

"Yeah." Mark and his mom are laughing.

"Give me ten minutes." The phone rumbles across the mouthpiece. I wait for something else. I get a dial tone.

❧

I kick off my shoes once I'm inside the door. Hang up my jacket. My dad pulls down a bottle of whiskey from the cabinet above the fridge. He throws some ice cubes into a glass and then fills it. The cubes pop as they crack. *At least he waited to start in on the hard stuff.* He stares at me. I head down the hallway. A sharp, chemical aroma fills the air. It's damp and thick and near my bedroom. I hesitate but open the door.

A smooth surface has replaced my wall that used to look like some demented kid's jack o' lantern. The joint compound is still wet in the middle. I walk back to the kitchen. My dad's still standing at the counter. I pull my kit out of my pocket and lay it down. I test. He doesn't flinch. He doesn't turn his back.

Part Two: Chronic

Chapter 10

Can such things be
And overcome our senses like a summer's cloud
Without our special wonder? (3.4.135-137)

Can I actually freeze my ass off? If so, could doctors re-attach it? I might need this surgery. The tradition of sending kids to sit and wait on the ground at the bus stop must stem from some adult envy. Parents and teachers always crack about how work is so much goddamn harder than school. This is our punishment.

But maybe work is worse. I know my mom was worn out when she came in both Saturday and Sunday mornings. Bags rolled out from under her eyes. She wasn't too exhausted to sit me down at breakfast, though. Read over my logbook. "Is this everything?" Then ask about my night. "So you and Sid had fun at Mark's?"

My Sunday morning reading was 336. She frowned. "The dawn phenomenon. We'll have to watch this." I didn't bother to ask what that meant.

I was 257 this morning. She chewed her lip. "You'll be fine." She's nervous. So am I. But with a reading that high all I could do was give my insulin time to work. Then inhale my breakfast right before I left. My mom hugged me and said, "Good luck."

Now I'm bloated and freezing at the bus stop. I shift my butt cheeks. Rock them like they've fallen asleep. It's Monday. I'm freezing.

Where the hell is Sid?

I figured maybe we could talk. I could get the truth. Maybe he'd tell me that he screwed up. Then it would be all good. But he still isn't here. Makes me wish I had gone through with calling him. I tried last night. I sat there with the phone in my hand. Six of the numbers pushed. I couldn't bring myself to hit the last one. Which was probably a good thing. My hand was shaking when I set down the phone. Then my stomach growled.

I tried to act all smooth. To get the glass and pour the juice like it was no big deal. Knocked my glass to the floor. The racket forced my dad to get up from watching TV. He told me to sit at the table. Poured me another glass of juice. Then he cleaned up my spill.

Still no Sid. I don't want to ride this bus alone. I'll be like a foreign exchange student with my new identity. Not the fun kind. Like the ones who are all polite and can almost speak the language, but pause at these weird intervals and say, "I'm not raffing at you." They're great. But me, no. I'm like some castaway kid who is a mess because his parents are alcoholics. Signed up just to get away. These kids barely sleep and it's against the law for them to shower. Honestly, I'm lost without Sid. Then again, even if he does turn up, I'm not sure I could face him.

The only seat left is next to Ted. This fat kid who smells like he's wearing a sweater made out of jock straps. I sit and hold my breath. Whispers slide up.

"Ed?"

"Yeah."

"Some disease."

"I don't know."

"Some sugar thing."

"What about your grandma?"

No one speaks to me, though. The bus pulls away. No Sid. I stare at the seat ahead of me.

We pile off the bus. I head to Mrs. Lee's office. I put my supplies on her desk. She refills her coffee mug.

"What was your level this morning?" She sips.

I take a quick look around. Nobody else is with us. "Two-fifty-seven." Mrs. Lee nods, but says nothing. I zip up my book bag and shoulder it. "See you before lunch." I turn.

"Ed?"

Mrs. Lee is doing that frowning-leaning-against-the-wall-staring-into-her-coffee move. She looks up. "Come back any time you need to. Don't be afraid to just raise your hand and ask. All your teachers are aware."

Aware of what? Aware that I'm scared out of my mind. That my best friend isn't talking to me. That I'm "disgusting." That my home life is a nightmare, with a dead uncle, worn-out mother, and emotionally-absent father. Oh yeah. I almost forgot. An incurable disease. Somehow one of the toolboxes here is supposed to know how to help me with this? Half these fools can't even speak to kids without it sounding like they swallowed a script.

I smile at Mrs. Lee. It isn't her fault. "Thanks." I move on to homeroom.

Mr. Stents teaches advanced math to the smart kids. They're actually going to make something of themselves. He's got pictures of them on the wall behind his desk. At math competitions and Intelligence Olympics. The same five kids.

I ignore the homeroom around me by staring at these smiling faces in perfectly pressed clothes. Someone next to me farts. Someone else laughs. The bell rings and the announcements come on.

I turn to the TV in the corner. I also look for Sid. His seat's empty. Silent Bob shoots me a look. But collapses back onto his desk like a squirrel with a nut. "Yearbook will meet after school, today. We will discuss possible layouts for our upcoming edition." The girl who is reading this from the kitchen-counter-made-to-look-like-an-anchor-desk is real popular. She's a cheerleader and in National Honors Society. More importantly, she's fantastically attractive. We all stand as she begins to recite the pledge. I'm saying, "indivisible, with liberty," and Sid rambles in.

Mr. Stents moves toward the door. Sid casts Stacy off his arm like he's removing a coat. She collides with the other two tarts out in the hall. Their laughter echoes as they walk away. Then it's just Sid moving across the room.

He looks off to the side. Laughter resounds. I look around. Everybody has returned to his seat. But me. I'm standing. Giving my own silent salute to Sid. I turn red and sit down.

Sid plops into his seat. Two up from me.

"Your pass?" Mr. Stents nudges his glasses up his nose.

"Don't have one." Sid shrugs.

"Well, did you sign in? You're late."

Sid sits upright. "Really? What am I late for?" He looks about the room. "Did something actually happen around here?"

The room laughs.

"Very amusing. Go sign in."

Sid slides out of his chair and is then out the door. He yells something. Startles Silent Bob. He drops his pen. Kids are packing up. I bend over and get the pen for Bob. He's real fat. Like Ted from the bus. But he doesn't wear jock strap sweaters.

I hand over his pen. Bob stares at me. He looks like that Punxsutawney Phil thingamajig. "It's like that now."

It's creepy how he says it. All deadpan. I lean toward Bob. "What do you mean?" He hesitates. Looks over his shoulder. Like he's paranoid.

"Sid and Stacy. You know?"

"Uh, not really. Like *what* now?"

Bob's mouth hangs open. The bell rings. Mr. Stents moves to the door. He smiles. Wishes us all a nice day.

I step into science. Set down my bag. I pull out my assignments and hand them to Mrs. Didi. She looks at me like she's peering into a microscope. "Ed Devlin. You know. Just got diabetes." Her shoulders ease. She leans back.

"O——oh, that's right." She pauses. "Well, that's fine." She turns away.

I head to my seat. Mark laughs. "Welcome back."

I shake my head. Take out my notebook. Mrs. Didi's at the blackboard. She clouds herself in chalk dust. Sid's up front. He ignores me. Slouches in his chair. The three-pack—Ashley, Brittany, and Stacy—turn around to look at Mark and me. They laugh. Ashley holds her nose and pretends to cry. Brittany balances a pencil on hers. Goes all cross-eyed looking at it. Mark lowers into his seat. Touches his splint. He opens his sketchbook and scribbles away. I zone out. I've got no comeback for the trio. It's only my first class and already my head's just too full for me to be able to do anything else.

❧

"You can have extra time to complete the essay." Pilsner smiles his patented frown.

"Thanks. Where are we in *Macbeth*?"

Pilsner laughs. "Have you been reading?"

I nod.

"Just no writing."

I nod again.

"We're reading Act Three, scene four this period."

"That's where I left off."

Mr. P eyes me. "You know, what you are experiencing now could teach you so many lessons. While at the same time make for one great story." I look at him to see if he's joking. He's one of those teachers who can be so sarcastic that it's difficult to know the difference between a joke and the truth. But he stands there with his lips all pressed into a tight line. "Seriously."

I head to my seat and there's a ruckus behind me. I turn. So does the rest of the class. Sid's at the doorway. Stacy in tow. He's got an arm around her waist. Her second-skin shirt has ridden up. Exposing the belly button ring and the faint outline of her bra. She grabs his rear and laughs. All open-faced and hinged-jawed. I sit near Mark. Sid takes a seat with the trio. Away from me. Silent Bob stares. He shrugs. I understand.

"This scene has to be watched to be understood" Pilsner rolls a TV to the front of the room. "I'm going to play it. But I want you to follow along in your books." We dig out our copies. Mr. P cues up the tape. Sid

83

and the three-pack slouch in their seats. Not a book amongst them. Mr. P clears his throat. "One question: Where's Banquo?"

The smart girl up front answers. "He's dead."

"Exactly. Remember that." Pilsner flips off the lights. "Act Three, scene four." He presses play.

That is ridiculous. Macbeth's got everybody over for a banquet. I mean *everybody*. Including Banquo's ghost. Oh yeah, Macbeth freaks. Screams at the thing, "Never shake thy gory locks at me." He's the only one who can see the ghost though. Crazy. Macbeth's crew busts out. Lady Macbeth tries to calm her husband down. It's eerily familiar.

Pilsner turns the lights back on. We all squint. Except Sid. He's sleeping. The girls look comatose. All spacey-eyed. "So now Macbeth's past actions are literally coming back to haunt him," Mr. P says. "Consider the lines, 168–170: 'I am in blood stepped in so far that, should I wade no more, returning were as tedious as go o'er.'" Pilsner looks over the class. "What does he mean?"

The class shuffles. Looks around.

"There's no point in turning back." Mark's voice is surprising and deep. I turn to him.

Mr. P smiles. "Absolutely."

Something moves across the room. I look over. Sid's not sleeping anymore. He's staring just past me. Mark meets his stare. Again, movement. Stacy leans on Sid's shoulder. She whispers in his ear.

The bell rings. I want to stay and talk to Mark. But I have to go to Mrs. Lee's. I walk to her office. Grab my kit. Test. My meter beeps: 322. *No.* Mrs. Lee looks up from the papers on her desk. "What are you?"

I pull out my logbook and grab a pencil. "Three-twenty-two." It's lunchtime. I'm starving. *What am I going to do in the lunchroom without food? Sit and watch other people eat?*

"Here's your Humalog." She passes over the insulin. I grab a syringe and an alcohol pad. "You've got your chart?" I nod. Mrs. Lee returns to her work. But she's eyeing me.

The needle stings. I didn't give the alcohol any time to dry. I wince.

Air rushes through my teeth. "You all right?"

"Yeah." I get up and drop my syringe in the large Biohazard container mounted on the wall. I consider climbing in with it and hiding there for the rest of the day.

"It will get easier, Ed. It's your first day back." Mrs. Lee stands. I shoulder my bag.

"I know." I look at my feet.

"Now, off to your next class."

"Huh?"

"It's not lunch yet. After *next* period."

I look at the clock. It's only 11 AM.

How did I manage this?

She moves toward me. "I was actually surprised to see you. I just didn't want to embarrass you by saying anything." She tilts her head. "But it's good. Because now maybe you'll be closer to normal for when you eat." She smiles. "Remember, no study hall after class. Lunch first."

"What do you mean?"

"Don't you remember? Monday, Wednesday and Friday. You're eating during the other lunch period."

"I am?"

"Remember? When you were here with your mother? You agreed."

What have I gotten myself into?

I walk into history late. Mr. Daniels opens his mouth. He waves me on. I sit next to Mark. "Class, turn to page 387." Daniels perches at his podium. He drones.

I try to focus on the lesson. But it's like a non-stop voice in my head: *Am I going higher? My stomach just growled. Maybe I'm low? No, that's just regular sweat. Nothing serious. No one's looking at me. No one cares. Damn I'm hungry. I wonder how my level will be in an hour? Who the hell eats lunch next? Will I be able to eat dinner on time? Maybe I'm really crazy and this is my body's way of showing it?*

Mr. Daniels clears his throat. I look up. He's standing before me with a stack of papers. "Oh." I reach out and take them. I place one in my left hand. Pass the rest back with my right.

"Ewww! Gross! Is that? Like blood? On my paper?"

I look back. The girl at the end of the row is holding her paper in the air. A red dot highlights the top. The kid in front of the girl holds up his. "Hey, it's on mine too." Then the kid in front of him. Then the rest. Up to me. I look down at my right hand. One of the miniscule scabs on my finger has come away. The blood has dripped into the webbing. Stacy yells, "Ed's bleeding!"

The other two beasts chime in. "Bleeding! He's bleeding!"

The entire class is staring at me. I'm boiling inside.

"Go see Mrs. Lee, man." Mark says. "Don't sweat this."

Mr. Daniels opens his mouth. I leave before he has the chance to ask me anything.

Mrs. Lee is standing by the bathroom in her office. "Well, you're going to have to let me come in and see. I can't help you from out here." There's a long pause. Then the pinched voice of some guy is muffled by the closed bathroom door. Mrs. Lee shakes her head. "I promise." The lock clicks in the door. The hinge squeaks. Mrs. Lee says, "Jesus, Mary and Joseph."

I sit next to her desk. She situates the kid from the bathroom onto a cot in the back. He moans. She crosses to me. "Don't ask. You really don't want to know." I peek around the corner. Like the saying goes, "misery loves company."

"Weren't you just here?" I show her my hand. The blood has dried and looks like the beginning of a stigmata. *If only I were so lucky.* "Let's clean that up." I follow her to the sink.

"I got it all over the papers in class." I scrub with soap and water.

"How so?"

I explain. I'm sure the rumor mill is churning out an entirely different story as I do: *And, like, he flipped off Mr. Daniels. And blood squirted from the top. And like I think you can like catch what he's got. Oh my God! Maybe that's why he did that! He should be expelled!*

Mrs. Lee frowns. Hands me a towel. Then a band-aid. "You've just got to pay attention to this kind of stuff now."

"All right." I throw out my towel. My stomach growls. The kid on the cot stops squirming. He sits up.

"What the hell was that?"

I ignore him and use my open wound to test. I apply the band-aid after. I imagine my fingers all taped up. Like some rugby player. Maybe I can get one of those jerseys with "Diabetic" stenciled on the back. My meter beeps: 122. "Thank God."

Mrs. Lee walks over. Looks at the meter. Smiles. The bell rings. "You ready to go eat lunch?"

I would like nothing more. Not even Mark's mom. "Please."

She shoots me a quick smile. "I'm glad you agreed to eat with the *special* students."

What? Special? Who does that mean... oh... no.

She means the handicapped. My school has this whole separate wing for them. The beginning of last year I got lost and ended up down there. The noises coming from inside the classrooms didn't strike me as abnormal, so I marched right into one. Thought I'd find my math class.

The room was full of kids. Painting. Drooling. Moaning. Their teachers circled among them. They smiled and said things like, "So what have you made here?" I was both frightened and filled with awe. Until one saw me and threw his paintbrush. I closed the door and a tumult ensued.

"Uh, that's okay. I can eat right here."

"No, Ed. Go down. You'll fit right in." Stacy steps through the doorway.

I cover my test kit. As if she's found me with my pants down. I stammer and cannot respond.

Mrs. Lee whirls around. "Is that rash back again?"

Stacy stammers. The kid on the cot starts laughing.

❧

I grab my lunch out of my locker and close the door. I round the corner. Guttural sounds echo from inside the cafeteria. I take the last few steps and open the door. There are three tables packed with lunch bags, wrappers and juice boxes. Surrounding the mess are fifty kids in wheelchairs. Or legs braces. Or giant coke-bottle-lens glasses. Some have adults sitting next to them. Feeding them. Others stare vacantly at the food on the trays attached to their chairs. I pause. The door slams behind me.

I move to a table at the far side of the room. I pull out my sandwich, crackers and diet soda. There's something white at the bottom of my bag. It's a note. I unfold the paper. My mom's handwriting. *Good luck honey. You'll be just fine. Remember, we love you.* It's signed, *Mom & Dad.*

I take a bite of my sandwich. Look at the special kids. Those who can are smiling. Clapping. Laughing.

Chapter 11

And that, distilled by magic sleights,
Shall raise such artificial sprites
As by the strength of their illusion
Shall draw him on to his confusion. (3.5.26-29)

I'M LIKE A NEW KID IN SCHOOL. Without all of the maybe-he's-some-bad-ass. Like they portray in the movies. The kids here look past me. As if they don't know who I am. This may simply be some consequence of my sugar-packed brain. Possibly it's misfiring and I'm not reading the signals like I should. I know that whenever I was with Sid people noticed me. Or at least they noticed me along with him.

But the evidence suggests things have changed. I'm sitting in the library. It's Friday. Last block. Kids are all clumped in groups. Not doing jack. No one has even glanced in my direction. I don't know where Mark is. But at least Sid and the trio aren't here. Rumors abound as to where they might be.

I've been catching up on the work I missed all week. Sid brought most. Not all. Which isn't all bad. It gives me something to do instead of looking like a reject. But most of the assignments suck. My teachers believe in keeping us busy in hopes that we might learn something.

I didn't mind finishing the essay about that one-armed hiker guy and *Macbeth*. The question was: *What similarities and differences exist between Aron Ralston's actions* (the hiker) *and Macbeth's? Consider how each man viewed his fate.* I wrote it after we finished Act Three. There's this scene in it where the head witch says, "He shall spurn fate, scorn death, and bear his hopes 'bove wisdom, grace, and fear." It wasn't hard to see the connection after that. The essay wrote itself: *Fate as a choice. Not just fate set in stone.*

Which got me thinking about myself, my dad and Uncle Brian. I wasn't sure if I should include those personal connections in the essay. But I finally said, "To hell with it!" I wrote about my dad and death and fate. I even threw in this nonsense with Sid, Stacy and Mark. Like I've heard my gramps say—only when tanked—"If they don't like the answer, they never should have asked the question." Pilsner was shocked at the five pages.

I'm working on some packet for History now. About some ancient civilization that actually got itself in gear and built a city instead of living in caves. But then they got wiped out by some army. It happens. *Maybe I should have ended my essay with that?*

I put my pen down and rub my eyes. They're heavy and dry. *Feels like moving a mouse that's got a stuck ball.* I look at the clock. Twenty more minutes. I wonder if my eyes are dry because I'm high. I've been high all week. It'd be nice if I were "stoned" high. Instead of this. At least I'd have a group to fit in with.

The bell rings. Kids charge from their seats like horses out of the gate. I shake my head to focus. Circle answers to the remaining questions without reading them. I pull all my crap into a heap and slide it into my bag.

I step out into the hall. Guys are flying around like someone just told them there's free food out in the parking lot. I go to my locker. Dump my load of papers and books into it.

"Hey, what's up?" Mark's standing next to me. Something's not quite right. I look over his shoulder. "You all right?" It's his voice. His real one. The one without the someone's-sitting-on-my-face tone. His splint's gone.

"I didn't realize it was you." I touch my nose. "No splint?"

"Yeah, I got it off this morning." He inhales extra hard. Flares his nostrils. "Feels good."

I shoulder up my bag. We walk down the hall toward our buses. "You got any plans for the weekend?"

"No. Nothing. You want to do something?"

I exhale. I absolutely do. I don't really care what. But my mom has to work this evening. My dad will be at the office working on his truck. "Yeah, but I don't have a ride."

"I'll come over."

"That works."

Sid isn't on the bus anymore. Either direction. I've overheard that Stacy's driving him. Or one of the trio is. Or something. She's seventeen. I'm not surprised. She seems like the kind of girl who would fail a grade and be proud of it. I've been getting my info from the kids on the bus. They don't really talk to me. Or to Ted. But they don't rag on us either. They seem to know a hell of a lot of stuff. Like now. This kid Pedro is talking about this web site where you can go and post your own stuff, for free.

"There's whacked stuff, yo. Bunch of heads from our school have pages. Crazy pics. You know?" He looks at me. I smile like I do. Pedro rolls his eyes. Ted rocks in his seat and pulls at his lips.

I'm walking home from the bus stop. My parents are standing by the kitchen window. Looks like they're talking. I watch for a second because it's a rare thing to see. Like a computer geek without glasses.

I walk in and set my bag by the door. My dad holds his mug of coffee. Stares at it. My mom bites back the words that are tumbling out of her mouth. "Everything all right?" I look at each.

My dad sets down his mug. "About tonight…" He doesn't finish, though. He looks at my mom. She looks at him.

For Christ's sake, what? I hang up my coat. "Mark's coming over."

"Oh," my mom says.

"That the kid whose house I picked you up at?"

"Yeah." I kick off my shoes.

"Sid, too?" "

I stare at my feet for a second. "He's got a girlfriend." This seems the safest route to take.

"Really, who is she?" My mom tilts her head.

A temptress with a belly button ring, surly disposition, and an air of superiority. "Just this girl. Stacy something-or-other."

My dad clears his throat. "You the third wheel?"

More like the flat on the side of the road. "Yeah." My parents exchange another look. I grab my bag and head for my room. "So it's all right that Mark's coming over?"

My mom answers. "Yes, but *we're* not going to be here."

"I know. That's why I invited him." My hand hits my doorknob. I twist but do not go into my room. My parents are whispering to one another.

I go in and crack out my logbook. It looks like this:

Date	11/23							Day	Friday													
	12A		5A	6A	7A	8A	9A	10A	11A	12P	1P	2P	3P	4P	5P	6P	7P	8P	9P	10P	11P
Glucose				225					215				179		302	181			256		
Carb				45					56							75					
Humalog				12					8						5	5					
Lantus				16																	
Exercise																					
Comments	I don't know what I'm doing. Diabetes can bite me.																				

It should look like this:

Date	11/23							Day	Friday													
	12A		5A	6A	7A	8A	9A	10A	11A	12P	1P	2P	3P	4P	5P	6P	7P	8P	9P	10P	11P
Glucose				115					85				97		110	115			122		
Carb				45					56							75					
Humalog				6					4							5					
Lantus				16																	
Exercise													1 hr								
Comments	Life is awesome. My diabetes is sooo under control. I'm thinking of running a marathon, and raising a million dollars for research.																				

I stare at the pages. Grab a pencil. I'm going to erase the "bad" readings and replace them with "good" ones. Why not? I put the eraser to the paper. I stop. *What's the point?* I walk back out to the kitchen.

My mom's at the table. It sounds like my dad is in the basement. I sit and slide the logbook to her. She grabs it and starts reading. A moment later she sighs. Really loud. "Jesus, Ed."

"That bad?"

My mom frowns and looks up. "It's not great." She looks back at the numbers. "We can tweak this, but…" She doesn't finish. My mom starts crying. Not heavy sobs or anything. Just a little trickle. I feel like I'm watching a private moment that isn't supposed to be seen. I get my mom a tissue. She takes it without a word. I sit down and wait. Noises continue from the basement: weights being racked. My dad's grunts. The rhythm of his counting. I want to go down there and smack him. *Why is he doing this to her?* But there's my logbook, lying open on the table. The horrendous numbers stare back at me. I can't only blame my dad.

That fact is unsettling. My mom's crying because of me. Not just my dad. Because of these lousy numbers. Because of my inability. Once again I don't measure up. Never will. But I'm not the only victim here. Sure it's my life that's been upended. But so have theirs. Especially hers. There's no other choice. I have to do better. I reach across the table and pat the back of her hand.

❧

My dad's just leaving. The doorbell rings. I open the door. Mark's standing on my porch with a sketchbook stuck under his armpit. "Hey, come on in." He does and comes face-to-face with my dad.

My dad scowls. Looks Mark up and down. "What's that?"

"It's my sketchbook." Mark sounds as perky as a cheerleader. My dad frowns. Crosses his arms over his chest. I tense up.

"Really? What do you draw?"

I'm staring at my feet now.

"Mostly people. But I paint too. So sometimes I sketch an idea for something completely abstract."

My dad gurgles. It's like the sound before someone vomits. He straightens up. "All right. I have to go. Ed, call me on my cell if you need anything."

I look up. But it's pointless. He isn't looking at me. He's out the door and I'm standing with Mark. "He seems nice."

I laugh out loud.

"What?" Mark sets down his sketchbook.

"Nice? Yeah, he's real nice. The two of you should hang out for a while so you can draw him."

"What's that supposed to mean?"

I laugh again. "What comes to mind when you think of the Incredible Hulk?"

"Angry. Green. Guy built like a Rottweiler."

"Just take away the green."

"Gotcha."

We go to my room. I'm embarrassed by how lame it is. My bed and floor and desk are all covered in crap again. I really don't know how this happens. I go to leave. But Mark's taking it in. Like he smells a fart. Something about his face reminds me of Ted. Which reminds me of what Pedro said. "Hey, have you ever heard of MySpace?"

"You mean the web site?"

It takes only five minutes to make an account and start searching. I don't know how this site hasn't been shut down. Every page we go to has kids appearing like they're auditioning for a role on *Cops*. Pedro was right. Lots of kids from my school have pages. But there's only one I'm looking for.

I type Stacy's name into the search field. In a flash she's on the screen. Posturing for the camera. She's got a message: "To all the girls out there interested in 'Sid Delicious'... stay away if you know what's good for you."

"'Sid Delicious,' huh?" Mark cocks an eyebrow.

I read more of her page. "Yeah, and she's 'Tasty Stacy.'"

"Perfect. I hope they eat one another."

I laugh and see that she's put her address on the page too. Twenty-two Fox Hollow. I point it out to Mark.

"Weird. Guess she's not afraid of stalkers," he says.

"Yeah. Or maybe she's hoping for some." I log off. Rub my face.

My mouth is dry. "You want a drink?"

Mark stands. "Damn right I do!"

Did I miss something?

We walk out of my room and to the kitchen. Mark turns on the TV and starts flipping through the channels. I grab my kit and test: 257. I have an urge to crush my meter. I picture the shards of plastic flying every which way. The screen clouding over with that inky, black residue. I cross to the fridge and get my insulin. I grab a syringe, alcohol pad and my coverage sheet from the drawer near the bread. My mom put it all there the other day.

Mark's at the counter. "Awesome. You're going to inject. Right?" I stare at him. Wait for the joke. None comes.

"Yeah, you... uh... you want to watch?"

"Hell yeah! I dig needles."

Who are you? I draw up three units. Wipe my stomach with the alcohol pad. Hold my breath. Bombs away. No pain this time. I pull the needle out. Mark smiles. "You rock. Thanks for letting me watch." I drop the syringe into the Biohazard container. "How about that drink?"

I open the fridge. "What do you want?"

"I'll take a beer if your dad won't notice. But I'm fine with liquor too."

My brain does a little somersault. My stomach flips. The rest of my body lurches. I've never really drank. I mean, I've taken sips from my dad's beer. I once got buzzed at my cousin's wedding. That's it. *Can I drink? Doc never said a word. But why would he?* I'm staring at a beer. Then I picture all the kids from MySpace. All the smiles. *One of those kids has to have diabetes.* Then, *I can't lose Mark too.*

The liquor cabinet is just above my head. My dad's had me get him bottles countless times. Especially during this past year. It's filled with tequila and rum. Whiskey and scotch. "It's probably best if we drink the liquor. My dad will notice the beer." I close the fridge.

"Fine with me. Where's it at?"

ꕥ

Mark's a pretty goddamn good bartender if I do say so myself. And I do say so myself because it's me talking and nobody else. Right? Damn. I'm hammered. I'm sitting in my dad's recliner. I just finished laughing so hard at this Snuggles commercial. That little bear who's always talking with little kids while he's running out in a field. He blabs about how "soft" all this crap is. Then he bounces and just floats in the air. I imagined wiping my ass with his soft little body.

I told Mark. His rum and Coke shot out his nose. Which got me laughing. I landed in my dad's chair and felt, as if for the first time, how awfully comfortable it is. I understand why he spends most nights in it.

Seriously though, Mark can make a good goddamn drink. He even cut up a little lime wedge and stuck a straw in the glasses. I think rum and Coke is the perfect drink for me. It's got like no calories. No carbs. Nothing. I didn't know that liquor had nutritional information on it. Or beer either. But Mark showed me where to find it on both. Now I've got this whole idea that I might drink a lot more often. Because damn. It's got nothing that I need to worry about. I just feel so much better. So much looser than I have in weeks. Hey! My lime wedge looks like a little green mouth smiling at me. "Hi little guy. How are you?"

"You all right?" Mark laughs.

"Yeah. Fine. Fine. Just talking to Mr. Lime over here. He's doing laps right now. But believes that he'll be ready for a little time out of the pool soon. He promises not to go back in until an hour after he's eaten."

"I'm getting my sketchbook."

He gets up. I stare at my drink. *Ice cubes are amazing!*

Mark's arm works furiously. I'm trying not to laugh. Not to move a muscle. That's what you are supposed to do when you sit for an artist. Mark's certainly an artist. What would you call me? Definitely not a model. I had that whole gaunt look-at-me-my-clothes-are-falling-off-my-body working for me a couple of weeks ago. But I'm gaining the weight back now.

I'm laughing. Just a little tremble. Like a leaf in the wind. I try to control it. I take a deep breath. That only makes it worse. When I suck in I sound like those kids I always see at the pool bobbing up and down while the lifeguard's yelling at them to get out. They just keep bobbing and bobbing, and there's nothing that the damn lifeguard can do. They know it. He knows it. Even the old guy at the pool who just wants to do his laps knows it. That's funny. I'm laughing hard now. I haven't felt this good in a while. Not since… everything.

Chapter 12

From this moment
The very firstlings of my heart shall be
The firstlings of my hand. And even now,
To crown my thoughts with acts, be it thought and
  done. (4.1.166-170)

M Y ALARM CLOCK POUNDS INSIDE MY SKULL. I roll over and grope for it. The blaring continues. I grab it. *Where's the off button?* The sound is piercing. I close my eyes and slam it down. It shuts off. *Thank friggin' God!* I lie back down. Something cool and hard is beneath me. I reach under my neck. My test kit.

What the hell? When did I? My head pounds. *Last night. The drinks. Oh hell.* I throw my legs over the side of my bed. Wait for the room to still. I test. The pounding is now a wave. Rising and crashing. Rising and crashing. My meter beeps: 176.

Where's Mark? I stumble down the hall. The morning light is harsh. He's not on the couch. Nor in the bathroom. No way he's in my parents' room. I lean against the wall. Close my eyes. *Did he leave last night?* I try to remember. My brain is dust. A tiny voice cries, "Water! Please give me water!"

The front door opens. I stumble. It's my mother. She looks at me, leaned up against the wall. Wearing nothing but underwear and a serious case of bed-head. "What's wrong?"

"Nothing." I scratch my head. Trying to look like I'm just thinking really hard. But the wave returns. I turn away. Slide down the hall using the wall for support. My mom hangs up her coat.

"Ed, are you all right?"

"Yeah." I make it to the counter. "Just a little low."

"Sit. Let me get you juice." She hurries to the fridge. I sit at the kitchen table. The lie tastes terrible. She sets apple juice before me. The taste is heavenly. She sits. "Your father still sleeping?"

For all I know, my dad came home during the night. Then he and Mark went out drinking. Seriously doubt it though. "Yeah."

"What did you and Mark do last night?"

I sip the remainder of the juice. "Just hung out."

Their bedroom door rushes over carpet. My dad emerges. He's bleary-eyed. Looks like he'd been up all night. He walks to the coffee pot. Gets the can. Piles grounds into the filter. My mom watches his back. He turns to us. Rubs a hand from the back of his neck to his face. "Long night."

"Yeah it was." My mom stares at the space before her.

I wait for my dad to make a comment. To say something about what it looked like when he came home. Nothing. The coffee pot drips. I make some toast and grab my supplies. I inject without making a scene. My mother goes to bed. My dad turns on the TV.

A piece of paper sits on my desk. Not some random 8½ by 11. One of Mark's sketchbook pages. I close my door and go to it. It's a picture of me in the recliner. Glass in hand. Talking to this little cartoon/alien thing that's sitting on the lip of my glass. My eyes are all bugged and my teeth look like gravestones jutting out of my mouth. I laugh and tuck it behind my computer. I crawl into bed and hope my breakfast stays down.

৵৶

I thought maybe Pilsner would lay off and let us watch a movie. I mean, tomorrow's Thanksgiving. No, on to Act Four, scene one. Pilsner stands up front. "Open to Act three, scene six. Starts on page 111." We find the page. He reads. "He shall spurn fate, scorn death, and bear/His hopes 'bove wisdom, grace, and fear./ And you all know, security/ Is mortals' chiefest enemy." Mr. P looks around the room. "After we read Act Four, scene one, I want you to tell me how Macbeth does just this."

Most kids stare blankly. Mark sketches. Sid and the floozies look particularly out of it. *Who am I to talk?*

This scene is demented. Full of disembodied talking heads and bloody babies. Yet, Macbeth is sure of himself, positive of what he has to do to remain king: kill and feel no remorse.

"The answer to my question?" Pilsner smiles. No one answers. He frowns. Pinches the bridge of his nose. "I'll give you one. Be careful what you believe." The bell rings.

"I still can't believe you were so bombed."

My face is hot. "I don't drink much."

Mark laughs. "Really?" We head toward the cafeteria. Mark agreed to eat with the special kids after I yelled at him for leaving on Saturday without telling me. We round the corner.

Sid and his now ever-present ladies flank him. They're laughing and wobbly. My heart pounds in my ears. Jumps back and forth between my temples. I look down until we're past. *This is so messed up.*

A peal of laughter echoes off the walls. Mark stops. I stop. Sid's smiling. His face is crazy. He's licking his lips and laughing. Totally on something.

"Did you say something?" Mark voice is low and calm. But nasty at the same time. They glare at him—even the girls—in spite of the fact that their eyes are swimming in their sockets.

"Maybe." Sid shrugs. He looks at Stacy. She smiles and licks her bottom lip. Sid takes a step forward. "So?"

No, no. We can't fight. I've just injected. I need to eat. Damn! I don't have a choice.

Mark laughs. "Well, why don't you repeat yourself. Like a man. To my face." He looks at Stacy. "Or do you need permission?"

Sid's back goes straight. Stacy set her face tight. She pushes him. He's now a foot from Mark.

"I said, 'How's your nose. Little boy?'"

Mark smiles. "About as good as your girl there. A bit busted. But gets the job done."

"Who the…" Stacy steps forward, swinging. Mark backs up. Sid grabs her. She shoves him again. "Get outta my way!"

Pilsner steps into the hall. "Hey! What's going on?" He strides toward us.

Stacy swears like the trash she is. The dubious duo stare. Apparently enjoying the trip. I turn to Mark. "Let's go." We bolt and don't look back.

❧

It's after midnight. I just tested: 237. *This sucks.* My levels are a goddamn guessing game. I hop online. I just have to see something. I Google "diabetes and alcohol." I get 18,200,000 hits. I go to the second link: *Alcohol tends to lower blood sugar and can cause hypoglycemia (low blood sugar).* I go back and click on the fourth link. I read: *Drinking alcohol may result in your judgement being impaired. Many of the early warning symptoms of hypoglycemia are mimicked by alcohol. Your friends may also mistake these hypoglycemic symptoms for effects of alcohol and may not seek help until you lose consciousness.*

I shut down my computer and head to the bathroom. Hopefully for the last time tonight. The TV is on. My dad's in his chair. His eyes are so vacant that there's no way he's taking in what's on the screen.

I finish up and return to bed. My mind races. Tomorrow. The food. My relatives. My parents. Sid. Mark. Alcohol. Diabetes. No, no more. I shut my eyes. All I can see is my father. *What am I thankful for? What is he?*

❧

The Macy's Thanksgiving Day parade is frightening. I'm amazed that more people haven't been killed by those enormous balloons. Garfield lazily drifts over the heads of thousands. I bet that his eyeball could take out an entire family.

My whole clan is coming over for dinner. My mom's in the kitchen rubbing Crisco all over the bird. My dad's out getting last minute stuff like canned cranberry sauce, rutabaga, and that onion dip crap that you put on top of green beans. *Who thought of that one?* I grab my meter and test. My mom pretends not to watch me. Like she's all into shaking salt and pepper up the turkey's butt. My meter beeps. I sigh. She quits pretending. "What are you?"

Hopeless. "Two-fifty."

She sets the bird down and places a wrist on her hip. Her eyes are dreadful. Even worse than that dip. Her face seems more lined than before. "Ed, I want you to go run."

Was that a foreign language? "It's 20 degrees out."

"I mean on your father's treadmill." She points at me. "You remember what Doc Stevens said?"

I do. But this is big. Enormous. Bigger than my mom's cousin, Janet who will barely fit into one of the chairs I'm leaning against. No one but my dad uses his equipment. Period. Not since Brian died. "But, uh... I'm not so sure."

"Your father and I have talked about this. He's okay with it." There's a little twitch to her eye. But that might just be from exhaustion.

I put on a pair of shorts and a t-shirt and go down to the basement. My dad has mirrors up all around the room. I guess that's how you're supposed to decorate a gym. Too much reflection for my comfort. I touch the handles on the treadmill like they're fragile antiques. I have to chuckle. *Really, how hard can this be?*

I turn the power on. I almost bite it. The giant black tongue whirls at light speed. My dad must think he's a hamster or something. I plant my feet on the sides. Check the monitor. Find the speed control. I lower it to a more normal, I'm-not-an-obsessive-compulsive-exerciser level.

This isn't bad. The little red blips on the monitor do the wave. It's fun. They're like a cheering section. I amp up the speed. They increase their homage.

I'm sweating now. Feeling the burn. But I notch it up one more time. The little red blips look at one another but still cheer. It's their job.

Holy crap! I've been on the thing for 45 minutes. I'm drenched in sweat and my legs are throbbing. I cut the power and hover over the tread until the speed is reasonable. I let it propel me off.

I'm standing behind the treadmill, breathing heavy. My reflection assaults me. But for the first time in a long while there's some real color to my face. That "healthy glow" they're always pitching on the cover of my mom's magazines.

❧ ❧

Ah, family traditions. You have to love them. Here's our Thanksgiving: My relatives arrive late and offer no apologies. They sit on the couch and complain about the weather and how tired they are. They munch on peanuts and watch my mom run around like some medic at a drive-by murder scene. They drink one, two, maybe ten drinks before settling into the meal. Once eating they crack coarse, politically incorrect jokes. When they go over as well as the rutabaga, they bring up the painful subjects that no one wants to discuss. They try to make amends over dessert and sober up before driving home. Pilgrims and Indians—I'm sorry, Native Americans—alike are rolling over in their graves.

Everyone's around the table: Gramps, my aunt Helen, her husband Stan and their bratty kids Jeffrey and Clark. My mom's brother Daniel and her fat cousin Janet. On my dad's side, my Gran and Grandpa. That's it. Used to be my Uncle Brian as well. Yet, my dad keeps looking at the door like he's expecting someone else.

"Jumpin' Jesus on a pogo stick! This looks scrumptious!" My Gramps leans in and kisses my mom on the cheek. She smiles. But looks like a smashed bag of chitlins. "Thanks, Dad." She looks around the table. "Please, dig in." They do. It's as if my mom's fired a starter pistol. Which is good because my cousin Janet was seconds away from stuffing the entire turkey into her mouth. Like a tic-tac. I hold back. I have to calculate what I'm eating. My mom told me I didn't have to measure out my food. "We can just eyeball it." When she said this I thought of Garfield and gave her a look of my own. I'll give her credit for the exercise helping, though. I tested before the crew arrived: 138. I'll take it.

The fray clears. I manage to get some turkey, a roll, and some mashed potatoes. I look up. My mom cocks her head toward the green

103

beans. I grab a scoop. Everyone starts buttering and salting. Sloshing gravy everywhere. My mom looks at my plate. Gives a short nod.

"Ed, you sure you can eat all that? What with your sugar and all?" Stan's lips are pursed. Gravy hangs off the bottom one.

What, no ethnic jokes, Stan? I've got a forkful of turkey in my mouth. I swallow. "Yeah, I think so." I lower my head but check the rest of the table out of the corners of my eyes. The little brats Jeffrey and Clark are laughing. My Gramps is shaking his head.

"He 'thinks' so." Stan wipes his mouth. He had five highballs before dinner.

"Trust me Stan. He's fine." My mom bites into a roll.

"Sure, sure, Kathy. I got ya. Just checking. That sugar… hoo damn. I've seen what it's done. Not pretty."

I get what he means. I imagine myself with no legs. There goes my appetite. A moment of awkward silence descends. Gramps clears his throat.

"I'm sure Ed's doing quite all right. Hell, he's too young to be worried about all that. And I'm sure my Kathy keeps him on the strict path. Right, Ed?"

I'm completely comfortable with ignoring the question and crawling under the table. I'll stay there for the rest of the meal. Even if that means I have to stare at Janet's varicose veins and indistinguishable knees. But I have to answer Gramps. "Um… yeah. I'm doing well. Thanks to my mom. At least that's what my doctor said."

Gramps smiles. My mom's eyes soften. Stan stares ahead. Probably trying to find another side to argue. But I used the word "doctor." No way can some truck driver dispute that. Jeffrey and Clark snarl and resume eating.

I finish my meal. I'm not stuffed like I usually get. I consider seconds. But some part of me pipes up: *Um, screwball, let's keep it real. You've got a disease. Be happy that you'll live. Don't go getting all greedy like Janet over there. Did you see the amount of stuffing she put down? Is something growing out of her back?* I chuckle and stand. I clear my throat to get my mom's attention. She's gabbing away with my Uncle Dan. Waving her glass of wine around. "Mom." I mumble. She just yaks, yaks, yaks. "Mom." A little louder now.

"No kidding. I didn't know that you did that. I was just telling my friend at work that I needed…"

"Mom!" Great. Now the entire table is looking at me. Even Janet's taken her eyes off her plate. But she's still got a fork to her lips. That doesn't count.

"What?" She sets down her glass.

How do I say this: What amount of insulin should I take? How many units? I'm thinking of a number between one and ten… "How much do I need?" They all cock their heads in the same way. Except Janet. She's unhinging her jaw. Preparing to swallow the carcass.

"Oh… um…" My mom seems startled back to reality. "Let's see, the roll was 36 grams. The potatoes another 26. The beans, 4. That's 66. Divide it by 20. Three and a half."

They're looking between us like we're some savant math pair. "Thanks." I make a quick exit to the fridge and then to my room.

I return. It's as if someone has hung road kill from the chandelier. Everyone's backing away but won't get up to take it down. My dad's got one hand on top of his head. The other is firmly planted on the table. Like he's trying to keep his brain from exploding. Stan's talking.

"Well, I don't know. I've never been through that, but it seems like almost a year later you might be doing all right. It's not like you didn't know it was coming." The room goes still.

My mom slides a hand across the table to my dad. If he sees it there's no acknowledgement. He just stares at Stan. Like the words are still coming out of his mouth. Stan sits back and sips his drink.

My Gramps clears his throat. "Well, now, Stan. Let me tell you. I lost my wife—God bless her dear heart—five years ago… and it still hurts, every day."

Stan sits up. "Yeah, but that's your *wife*. This is his *brother* we're talking about."

"No, Stan. *You* are the one talking about him. Unless you got some mouse in your pocket." My Gramps sits back and crosses his arms over his chest. His face is crimson. His eyes are watery. He puffs his cheeks. Then he pats my dad's knee. It's a gesture I've never seen him do. I look over at my Gran and Grandpa. They've got the same matching, hollowed-out look. I've seen the same one on my dad too many times this past year. My heart sinks.

My dad collects himself like a ship gathering its sails. He breathes deeply. He moves his arms across his chest. My mom pulls her hand back. "I'm only going to say this once, Stan, so listen." He waits until Stan has given his full attention. Eyes locked with his. "Don't you ever tell me how to feel—not about my brother. You have no business having *any* opinion about him."

"Tim, I understand what you're saying, but…"

My mom places a hand on Stan's arm. "You're done with this conversation."

There's an awkward shuffling. Then everyone is nice. Too nice. Like we're strangers-trapped-in-an-elevator nice. Stan drinks his highball and his sons eye the desserts. My dad looks vacant. His pain radiates like the heat wafting off Janet's body. But I'm not repulsed by my dad. In fact, I feel sorry for him.

But, I don't know. As much as I don't want to give him credit, Stan's got a point. *Is my dad choosing this misery?*

I stare at the tablecloth. Now spotted with stains. My legs ache from my run. I'm tired. But in that you-know-you've-done-your-body-some-good way. I remember how I looked in the mirror. I also remember my last test result.

My mom's clearing the table. She chats easily, but sneaks a glance at my father. I look down at my hands. *Happy Thanksgiving!* They need more space. More time. That way my mom can heal my dad. I mean, it's what she does. She's a nurse. I'm never going to be the same again. I get this. But that doesn't mean I can't do what I have to do to get "better." If I figure out how to take care of my wound, maybe theirs can finally heal.

Chapter 13

But cruel are the times when we are traitors
And do not know ourselves; when we hold rumor
From what we fear, yet know not what we fear,
But float upon a wild and violent sea
Each way and more. (4.2.22-26)

PILSNER'S IN THE FRONT OF THE ROOM, yammering on about us needing to connect more with the literature we read. "I have a perfect example of what I mean right here." He holds up my essay. I slide down in my chair. I know it's mine because of the ridiculously slanted handwriting. I can't help it. I write like my words are trying to dive off the page.

I look around the room. Sid looks stoned. He has his hand on Stacy's leg. She doesn't seem to notice. The other two are concentrating on breathing. Mark is buried in his sketchbook. "Ed, would you mind coming up here and reading this to the class?"

At the beginning of the year Pilsner had this girl read her "getting to know you" essay. The one we wrote on the first day of school. He said her writing was "filled with exquisite details." Apparently dilapidated trailers, empty cupboards and a lunatic mother are exquisite. The girl started skipping class the next week.

I understand how awful she must have felt. *No. No I don't want to read about my life!* "Uh… no, that's all right. Just throw it out." My voice cracks. Someone laughs.

"Ed. Please." Pilsner's looking at me with that same concerned/hopeful/pensive face. I look over at Mark. He shrugs. I swallow and stand. The room perks up.

The paper shakes in my hands. I ignore the whispers and chuckles that pop around the room. More than anything, I avoid looking at Sid and Stacy. *Run you idiot!* But I can't.

I stare at the words. I clear my throat. I begin: "Fate, is it some pre-ordained script we follow? Or is it really just the luck of the draw? I am apt to believe that it is not just one or the other, but some combination. I have seen a strong, seemingly healthy man die. Personally I have pulled a marked card. Two uncontrollable situations. Yet both may reveal more about the life we choose to live than the life that has been chosen for us."

I feel like I'm in a tunnel. Everything is compressed into a tight circle of space. I keep my head down. Lick my lips. I silently read the next lines.

"I have a friend and a father who could both stand to learn this lesson. However, I'm afraid that neither is aware of his problem. Or more likely, knows how to deal with it." I looked up. Sid is staring at me. Not quite vacant anymore. Stacy's hand is cupped over her mouth, holding in a laugh. My stomach squirms. My heart leaps into my throat. I hand my paper back to Mr. P. "I can't. I'm sorry." I leave before he can speak. I head straight to the bathroom.

♋

Do miracles really happen? I'd seriously like to know. Because if they do I'll get down on my knees right now and start praying to any god who will listen. First, I want everyone who was in Pilsner's to forget my reading. But that's highly unlikely. Therefore, I'll settle for a new body. I'm skinny and scrawny. Even if I lift like my dad and eat a small child a day, I won't ever get ripped. I'm more like my mom—all nervous energy and thin arms. Anyway, I want a new body because—yes, obviously my pancreas crapped the bed. But lately, now that I'm trying to take care of myself on my own, I've been wondering about what else has been affected.

I just had a low in P.E. We were playing volleyball. It was great because Sid and the trio are out sick or whatever. Which meant that I got to hang out with Mark and didn't have to worry about getting served in the back of the head.

But I went all wobbly when it was my turn to serve. I tried to grip the ball and dropped it. Three times. Finally, I held the ball up over my head, but couldn't figure out how to release it while at the same time get my other arm to come up and smack it. My body washed out. Like someone came along and flushed my internal toilet. Clammy sweat covered my back. My heart thrummed. I set the ball down and my class groaned. Mr. Miner plucked the whistle out from between his teeth and said, "Nurse. Go."

I stumbled into the hallway and was harassed by a kaleidoscope of horror. It's almost Christmas. Therefore, the entire school is adorned in "festive" decorations. Everything from those torture device-looking menorahs. To over-excited Santas. To secretive looking snowmen. Seriously, there's this one that looks like he's lurking behind a snow bank just waiting to attack. Mrs. Lee saw me tottering in the hall and dragged me into her office.

She tested for me: 47. Now I'm sipping a juice box and lying on a cot. I started listing my ailments while floating in the twilight between low and normal blood sugar. I've got bruises and welts on my stomach from my shots. A still-svelte, yet sickly frame—even though I gained back seven of the fifteen pounds I lost. Dark circles under my eyes make me look like I stay up all night watching TV or surfing online. In spite of all my efforts I just don't sleep well anymore. I'm up most nights. Either high or low. Pissing or stuffing my face. However, there have been occasions when I've been up and my dad hasn't. Not often. But hey, it's some improvement. At least for him.

Therefore, for Christmas, I've got one item on my list: a new body. If you're listening, God, make it one with a nice set of pecs.

~ఌఄ~

I walk through the cafeteria doors and find my usual seat. Mark's not with me. Once was enough for him. He'd rather spend this time down in the Art wing anyway. I understand. Hell, if I were half as talented as him they wouldn't be able to get me out of there. I'd chain myself to a table. Or maybe paint myself to blend into the background. Like a chameleon.

The kids are looking at me. I mean they always glance over. But they also stare at their garbage from time to time like it's talking to them: *So, you like this new wrapper design? I'm not sure it complements my figure.* I finish half my sandwich. This one kid pops a crooked hand over his mouth and then scrambles underneath his table. I resume eating and frown at my celery stalks.

Compared to the regular cafeteria. Where like 400 kids scream non-stop for 45 minutes and fling their trash at one another. I'll take the squawking communication and drool-strewn trays from the special kids any day. I also like it here because I don't have to talk about diabetes.

During regular lunch I sit by myself or with Silent Bob. I once sat with some of my old acquaintances. All they did was diss my lunch and grill me about my disease. It was hard enough watching them stuff down Oreos and potato chips. And anything with a Little Debbie label. But having to explain why I really shouldn't eat any of it was just too much to stomach.

I'm done. I crumple up my bag so I can toss it like a basketball. I've already got the running commentary: *After a dashing burst of speed, Devlin's down the court. The clock's ticking, almost up, but what's this… someone with a… Christmas gift?* One of the kids is at my table. He's leaning on a crutch. With his free hand he's holding a package. I stare like a foreigner unsure of the native customs. The kid pushes the package forward. His crutch clinks off the table. "Merry Chrimas."

Grab the damn gift! I do. Smile and say, "Thanks."

The kid hobbles away. I look past him. The rest are watching. Even the one who went into hiding. I tear off the gift-wrap. Pull the top off the box and push aside the tissue paper. Inside, folded and arranged so that I can read it, is a bright yellow t-shirt: "Normal is an odd word." Underneath: "East District High Handicapped Alliance." The tears sting the back of my eyes. I stand and hold the shirt. It unfurls before me like I'm showcasing it. The applause starts. Soon the room is filled with the clanging of braces and the awkward connection of bent hands. Celebrating.

∽∾

I tuck the shirt into my top drawer. Tomorrow's the last day before break. I won't have a chance to thank the special kids. Get them cookies or doughnuts or something. *Next year.* I chuckle. I hate that expression: "See you next year!" It's only like ten days.

I change into my running gear. I'm trying to run three times a week. It helps my sugars. That's been obvious. But it also gives my parents some time to be alone. At least when their schedules align.

I flip on the TV and start stretching. Oprah's on. Something about "real life" miracles. I laugh into my knees. The door opens and I hear my mom's voice. "What are you doing?"

I turn. "Just stretching." She cocks an eyebrow. "I'm going on the treadmill."

But she's not looking at me now. The TV's beeping. The message scrolls across the bottom of the screen: *Winter Storm Warning. 6-10 inches of snow expected by the morning commute. Snow will be heavy at times. Total accumulation: 12 inches. Parents should advise their children against going outside, for fear of a possible "stalker" snowman on the loose.* It doesn't say that last part. But it could.

"Well, your father will be happy," my mom says.

I hope so.

My run was awesome. Those little red blips sure can get grooving. They motivate the hell out of me. I get a drink of water and stare at the Christmas tree. In spite of my mom's Martha-esque flavor, our tree is still a hodgepodge affair. It's adorned with random ornaments from gifts and from the decorations I've made throughout the years. Like the one with a picture of me as a baby. Glued to a Styrofoam circle. Surrounded by garland and speckled with green glitter. Priceless. My dad's truck sounds in the driveway.

"Hot damn! Makin' some money tonight!" He practically skips

through the door. He looks at me. "No way you're going to have school tomorrow. Now, *there's* a nice Christmas gift!" I smile. He crosses the room and then turns back. "Where's you mother?" I point toward the garage. He looks over. "All right. I've got calls to make. If she comes out let her know I'm home." My dad takes off to his bedroom, happy as an elf. I look out the window. On my neighbor's lawn there's a kid decked out in his snowsuit. He's holding a sled and looking up at the sky.

܀

The phone rings. I answer because my dad's long gone. He made about twenty calls and then took off to his office. My mom's still in the garage. "Hello?"

"Ed, is that you honey? How are ya?" It's my mom's friend from work, Christine.

"I'm all right. You want to talk to my mom?"

"Well, you and me could just shoot the bull if you'd like, but I doubt you want to hear about my depressing love life." She's always like this. Talks like a trucker and is waiting to live in a soap opera. Which would be cool. Everyone is good looking and loaded. And you can come back from the dead.

I open the door to the garage. My mom's in a pool of pictures and fabric and little doo-dad decorations. She startles like I've fired a gun. "What is it?"

"Christine's on the phone." I extend the cordless to her.

My mom sits back and takes a breath. "Well, did she say what she wanted?" I shake my head. She sighs and takes the phone from me.

Five minutes later my mom's getting her stuff together for work. "Just heat up some leftovers. Call me if you have any questions." She's breezing through the house just like my dad was. But she's not happy. "I want you to make sure that you test before you go to bed." She stands next to me. I'm slouched in the recliner watching the Doppler radar expose a cancer of a storm moving up the coast. "You got me?" The hospital expects all sorts of accidents because of the people travelling. She doesn't want to leave me alone. But she has no choice. She isn't stupid.

She knows I'm trying. But that I'm still a mess.

"I'll be fine. Promise." Then I have an idea. "I'll call Mark. See if he can come over. Maybe stay." She smiles at this. Kisses the top of my head.

❧

Mark's smiling when he walks through the door. He's holding a sketchbook. He's got his backpack on. "You ready for a winter blitz?" I shrug. He holds a finger in the air. Drops his bag and unzips it. Pulls out a bottle of rum and hands it to me. My heart thumps. My breath catches. Mark crosses the room and grabs two glasses. I swallow and compose myself.

❧

"Winter Wonderland" is playing on the radio. I've got the weather channel on. It's 7:00 and I've had two rum and Cokes already. The world is a warm, toasty place. Mark's staring at the Christmas tree. He drinks and sways. "You were a fat baby!"

I know just the ornament he's looking at. I'm like ten months old. At some family picnic. Sitting in a sandbox. Not just some rectangular thing. No, one of those old-school ones, shaped like a turtle. Complete with a shell for the lid. Fantastic! Anyway, in the picture I'm sitting up, staring at some shiny object or something. I look like Buddha. I was literally swollen everywhere. I had cankles. Just like Janet.

I go make another drink. My initial fear wore off after the first one. I'll be fine. I offer to make one for Mark. He just holds up his half-full glass. I slide ice cubes into my own glass. There's this sign at the local fire station: *No ice is safe ice.* I want to bring them a couple of cubes and ask, "How about these?" They'd probably punch me out.

"Your dad plowing?"

Mark's voice sounds weird. Like it fell down into his chest as he tried to speak. It strikes me that I don't know one thing about his dad. I know everything about his mom: She's 5' 7", 130 lbs. Wears a 36 C-cup and a size four waist. She has a smile that could dazzle the pants off anyone. "What's your dad do?" I'm heading back into the living room and this real sappy song—something by Bing Crosby—starts playing.

Who names their kid Bing?

"He's… uh, in design. Creates crap for ads and whatnot." He looks away. "My dad split about a year ago. Right after New Year's. My mom and him had this big fight." He sips his drink. "I'm not even sure what it was about." Mark sits in the recliner. Smooth as silk. I aim for the couch and bang my ass on the arm. "They both sat me down and told me that I'd understand. Someday." Mark sighs and looks down at his feet. "Still haven't figured that one out."

This is hard to believe based on the pictures in his house. But hell, appearances can be deceiving. *Isn't that the truth?*

The music blends with Mark's story and it's just sad. The blue light from the television and the multi-colored glow from the tree paint the room in a depressed hue. "That sucks. I didn't know."

Mark shrugs. "It's all right." I look at the television. He extends his arm and clinks my glass. "Merry Christmas."

I sip my drink and look over at my tree. My bright yellow Pokeman ornament glows. *Now I've got my yellow shirt.* I laugh out loud.

"What?"

I laugh again. "Hold on." I scramble to my bedroom. Change into the t-shirt. I look at myself in the mirror and am almost blinded by the banana-yellow glow.

Mark's leaned back in the recliner, staring out the window. He almost dumps his drink on the carpet when he sees me. "Where did you get that?"

"Nice, huh?" I pull the corners so he can read it better.

"No kidding? The kids you eat with?"

I nod and we both start laughing. I lean on the couch because I can't breathe. "Rockin' Around the Christmas Tree" starts playing. I turn it up. Outside, tiny snowflakes fall. Adding to the coating on the ground.

୧୨

Something isn't right. For real. Something is pretty far from all right. I'm numb all over. My eyes have tucked themselves way back in my head. I'm in a tunnel and everything sounds muffled. The music's playing but I can't tell what song. Mark's asking me a question. But I can only see his lips moving. My heart flutters like a butterfly. Not one soaring, mid-flight one. One with a wing pinned to a board. Struggling to regain flight without tearing itself.

My head lists like I'm on a ship. My brain screams for air. I open the door and stand on my front porch. The sky is filled with cotton balls plummeting to the ground. Little parachutes flutter across the streetlights. The kid across the way isn't out. Most of the homes are dark. Except for their Christmas lights. It's late. I'm cold. Something just isn't right.

Mark's behind me. Saying something. His hand is on my shoulder. I shrug it off. I lumber back inside. My legs are like concrete. I grab my kit off the counter. Spread it open. I fumble and drop the vial of strips. Mark picks them up. Hands them over. I manage to get one into the meter. My hands shake. I draw the lancet pen to my finger. The pop. Then the blood. But I can't get it to the strip. Mark holds my meter and brings it to my gyrating finger. The screen changes. Begins to count back. Mark looks between the screen and me. I go to speak. My meter beeps: 27.

"Get off me!" My arms and legs are tied down. Someone is holding my head. Jelly slides across my tongue and fills my cheeks. I spit. "Get that out of my mouth!" I strain past the hand on my forehead. "Let me up!"

The hand pushes me back down. Another joins it at my jaw. This one holds my mouth open for the jelly. Then clamps it shut until I swallow. I groan like a caged animal. No words. Just guttural moans. I flail until my shoulders are hot with pain. I squirm and someone pushes a needle into my arm. I lurch again. But too many hands are on me. The pain is obliterating. Coursing from my arm to my spine and ricocheting throughout my body. I cry out. My voice echoes off the walls.

"Ed? Hey, Ed? Are you in there?"

I open my eyes. It's like coming out of a dream. Doc Stevens is in my face. "Hey, there he is. Thanks for joining the party." Doc smiles and steps back. My mom, my dad, Mark, his mom, a nurse, and two guys in white with thick arms, stand along the wall at the foot of the hospital bed. Their faces are all the same. Horrified. As if I've just shown them some disturbing trick that I can perform with my posterior. I look from them and across my body. Restraints hold my ankles and wrists. There's a stain across my t-shirt. A puncture wound dots the crook of my arm. My head swims. A dull ache forms inside my skull. I stare into the white light above me. I will it to burn out my eyes so that I don't have to cry the tears that I know are about to stream forth.

Chapter 14

Give sorrow words. The grief that does not speak
Whispers the o'erfraught heart and bids it break. (4.3.246-247)

"E D. HEY. IS IT ALL RIGHT THAT I CALLED?"

My parents told me that Mark was not allowed to come over. They didn't say I couldn't talk to him. "Yeah. It's fine. You all right?"

"*Me*? I'm fine. What about you?"

The guilt is still a weight around my neck. It tugs every time I test. Or inject. Or write a reading in my logbook. "I'm good. No permanent damage or anything."

"Good. Because that was messed up. I thought you were just hammered. Until you tried testing." He pauses. "I don't know jack about where your whole blood level is supposed to be. But the last clear words from you were after you looked at that screen. You said, 'Something isn't right.'"

"Really?" I sit down at my desk.

"Yeah. How much do you remember?"

The weight tugs. "None of it."

"No shit?"

"Yeah. Total blackout. We drank. I woke up in the hospital."

Mark whistles. "You want to hear it?"

It's like watching the blood being drawn from my arm. I don't want to. But some twisted part of me has to. "Let me have it."

Mark clears his throat. "All right. So the first thing I did was call

117

9–1–1. It was just like on TV. They took the address and all that. Then kept talking to me until the cops got there. I had to describe what you were doing."

"What was I doing?"

"A pole dance around your Christmas tree."

I close my eyes and moan. *No wonder it was so crooked when we got home?* "Heh. I'm just getting started. So the cops roll up first. You started jumping up and down saying 'I bet it's a warrant for my arrest,' and, 'My mouth's bleeding!'" Mark laughs. "What movie is that from?"

"*It's a Wonderful Life.* My mom watches it every year."

"Yeah. That's it. Well you even hugged one of the cops and said, 'Zuzu's petals. Zuzu's petals!' Then the ambulance came on the scene. The cops were happy to get rid of you."

I imagine this scene. The mayhem. The middle of a snowstorm. I wouldn't be surprised if our neighbors move away. "How'd you get to the hospital?" *I at least remember that.*

"I had to go with the cops. They wanted to know about the rum."

"Really?"

"Yeah. My mom's pissed."

Does she look even hotter when angry? "Sorry about that."

"I'll live. So the cops followed the ambulance to the hospital. When the medics pulled you out, your pants were around your ankles."

"What?"

"And you were singing 'Jingle Bells.'"

"Jesus."

"I know. It was great. They pulled your pants up and brought you into the E.R."

"How'd that go?"

"You hopped up and down on the chairs until someone went and found your mom."

My heart sinks. "I didn't know they got her."

"Yeah. One of the nurses." Mark's voice is soft. "She showed up and called your name from across the room. You froze. Then started crying and apologizing. Some kid with a broken leg laughed. You went after him. That's when the orderlies dragged you into a room."

I so owe my mother an apology. I don't think my lame Christmas gift is going to make up for this.

"Best part. Before you freaked out when they gave you an IV and that gel, the cop pulled me aside and asked about your shirt."

"What do you mean?"

"He thought that you were... you know... special."

"Damn." Mark laughs. I don't.

"Ed, I'm sorry, man. I got you into that mess. Getting you all tanked. It's my fault."

The weight tugs. "No, it's mine. I knew better." I sigh. Close my eyes. Unreal. Man I screwed up. A thought surfaces. "Did you draw any of it?"

"Of course."

"Wrap up the best one and we're even."

"All right." He laughs.

"Merry Christmas." I hang up and move to my bed. I remember the morning after. My conversation with Doc.

"How's my drunken sailor," he said, and came bopping into the room. He may just be the happiest man alive. For that and for his celebrity-good looks, I wanted to slap him silly.

Doc checked my results. "Some night, huh?"

I shrugged.

"What were you drinking?" Doc sat on the squishy-topped stool. "Beer?"

I sat up in bed. "Rum and Cokes."

"Well, you're no lightweight." Doc cringed to his left. Like the tag to his shirt was biting his neck.

"I guess not."

He wheeled closer to me. "Ed, I'm just going to cut to the chase. You screwed up. We all got that." Then he leveled his stare. "The question, now, is what are you going to do?"

I opened my mouth to answer. Nothing came. I just sat there. *I'm going to keep testing and taking my insulin and living the fun, fun, fun life with diabetes. What else?*

"You've got to make a choice. I'm sure you realize that. This isn't fun and games."

I actually pictured a board game. Like Monopoly. It had little hospitals to buy instead of hotels. An insulin vial and a syringe instead of the little doggie and the shoe. There wasn't a "Go to Jail" card. But rather a "Get an Amputation." I chuckled.

"Something amusing?"

Damn. His tone could have been used as a scalpel. He cut right through my goofy imagination. "No. No, I hear you. I was just thinking about…" but I didn't finish. I looked away. "I'm trying Doc. Really."

"Getting drunk during the middle of a snow storm is trying? Explain that."

"I know. I screwed up, but…"

Doc leaned in. "But what?" His tone was softer.

I thought about telling him how stupid I felt. How wretched my life's been at home and at school. How I didn't have a choice—my only friend now is Mark. I'd have shot heroin if that's what he was doing because I'm scared and lonely and weak. I wanted to tell him how I hate this stupid disease. How I have a dead uncle and a dad who might as well be. I wanted to ask him if he could fix all that with his bright smile. Could he get my parents to sleep in the same bed—hell, get my dad to sleep at all—and keep my mom from crying at night? Could he rearrange the stars so I at least have a fighting chance? But I knew the answer. I swallowed and said, "It's just hard."

Doc squeezed my shoulder and dipped his head. "I know, Tiger. It always will be."

Part of me hopes that Doc is wrong. But the vast majority knows he's 100% right. This isn't comforting. It just is. My parents didn't expect this. Didn't believe for a second that Brian would be dead. That my dad would be messed up. That I'd be sick. No one's got a crystal ball or is hearing any prophecies. And even if they did, what could be done about it? Some things you choose. Some are chosen for you. Either way, you have to deal. Or give up. Maybe I'll just write those two sentences. Hand them in. See if Pilsner makes me read that.

❧

Christmas morning. The gifts are all unwrapped. We're just sitting around the living room. My mom liked the sweater I got her. My dad said his work gloves were exactly what he needed. I got some running gear and an iPod. Along with underwear and whatnot. I didn't get the new body I wanted. No real shocker there. I've never heard that Santa was like the Jackson family

My parents are drinking coffee. I'm drinking tea. I like it, whatever. It's all very quaint. Very calm. For once. My sugar level was fine when I woke up: 149. Outside is still white from the ten inches that fell.

"I've got one more gift." My mom sets down her mug. Shoots my dad a look. Gets up from the love seat. She goes to the garage. My dad looks at me. I don't have a clue. I've been too busy finding the bottom of a bottle to know what the hell my mom has been up to.

He sits up straight. He repeatedly rubs his knees. If he starts rocking back and forth he'll look like this one special kid at school.

My mom returns with a gift the size of a shirt box. She places it in my dad's lap. Perches on the edge of the couch.

He hesitates, but then rips into the paper. His forehead crinkles. His head sinks into his shoulders. He swallows. But does not speak. He stares at the present: a scrapbook.

I edge over so I can see. It's a biography of my dad and my Uncle Brian. My dad turns the pages. He still doesn't speak. There are pictures from when they were in diapers. When they were goofy-grinning kids at school. When they were football stars in high school. There are pictures and little memorabilia from their fishing trips and vacations. All the holidays. There's even a page for my baptism. My Uncle Brian's grin is enormous.

There's one last picture. I have no clue how my mom got it. It must have been taken just days before my uncle died. Brian got real hollowed out at the end from the chemo. So did my dad. From the stress and not eating. At least that's what my mom says. The picture is a shot of my dad hugging Brian around his shoulders and neck. My uncle's face is sunken. He's bald. He has no eyebrows or eyelashes. Both he and my dad have their eyes closed. At first glance it's impossible to tell who is who.

"I... don't know what to say... to you right now." His voice is so fragile. So vulnerable that I have to look at the floor. I can't see him like this.

"I didn't mean to upset you..." My mom's voice is high-pitched. Wavering like a dying bird. He stands. He doesn't look at either of us. He holds the scrapbook and walks down to the basement. My mom follows but stays at the door. I sit on the couch and stare at the Christmas tree.

๛

I pick up the phone and dial Mark's house.

"Talk to me, Ed." Christmas music blares in the background.

"Mark?"

"Hey, how's it going?"

"How'd you know it was me?"

"Caller ID. We finally got a phone with the display." The music cranks. "Sorry about that. My mom's installing surround sound."

I have the urge to ask what she's wearing, but don't. I'm not sure that I could handle it. "You doing anything tonight?"

The music stops squealing. "No. Why? Are you allowed to see me again?"

This sounds so queer. "No. Yes. I'll just meet you out. I have to get out of here."

"All right. Let's go downtown. See who's around."

My dad's in the basement. That's pretty much where he is. All the time. Either there or work. Fortunately, I used the treadmill while he was out salting. I'm really flying down there. Maybe I'll get one of those runner's highs. But with my luck I'll get addicted. End up like some poor gerbil in its wheel. Unable to stop until I fall off.

My mom pulls into the driveway. I go to the window. She turns

122

off the car and just sits. *Is she listening to a song?* No. The keys are in her hand. I turn away and test: 119.

My mom hangs up her coat. Sees me. "How are you?"

"Doing fine. One nineteen."

She half-smiles. "Make sure you write *that* down." She pats my hand. Then she tilts her head, listening. "He in the basement?" I nod. "I'm going to go lie down." She pads down the hall. My dad grunts. The lock clicks on my parents' bedroom door.

I pick up *Macbeth* and read Act Four, scene three. I have time to kill, and Pilsner told us to finish the play over break. I don't know why I'm bothering. After the fool he made of me. I'm also probably the only one who will actually read. Maybe Mark will.

Well, the guy whose family got whacked is teaming up with one of the dead king's sons to go kill Macbeth. Macbeth's wife is sleepwalking, talking to herself about the murders and rapidly losing her mind. It's no wonder Mr. P has us reading this on our own.

My dad rumbles upstairs. I head to the kitchen. He's raiding the fridge.

"Can you bring me downtown?"

He pulls out lunchmeat and mayo. "When?"

"Whenever works for you."

He shuts the door. Grabs a loaf of bread. "I have to check on a client in a couple of hours. We'll go then."

"Great. Thanks." I wait but he turns his back and walks to the table.

❧

I'm standing on the corner downtown, waiting for Mark and freezing my rear off. Sadly, this seems to be a real pattern for me. My dad didn't even ask me why I wanted a ride. Why I wanted to be left on a random corner. Or who I was meeting. Neither did my mom.

I feel like one of those watch dealers in the city. The ones who assault you as soon as you step off the bus or out of a cab. "You like Rolex? I got Rollies for ya. 'Bout Movado. The ladies love Movado. 'Course they real. Twenty-four karat." My coat is packed with goods: test kit, insulin, syringes, alcohol pads, lancets, cereal bars and glucose tablets—these nasty, chalk-like, sugar-on-steroids stuff that I have to take if I go low. My mom put them in my stocking. Unlike the watch dealers, I doubt anyone wants to buy this stuff.

"Ed?" Mark walks up from the corner.

"Hey!"

"You look better than the last time I saw you." He punches me in the shoulder.

I chuckle. "Thanks. But you still look like crap." We both laugh and Mark starts walking. I follow.

"I want to check out this coffee shop up the way. It's supposed to be all new-age/hippie." He stops, turns to me. "You can drink coffee, right?"

So, what, we're joking about this, now? But his eyes are teasing around, pleading. "Coffee's fine if I use fake sugar. But I like tea better."

We head to the shop. It's all decked out in hemp products and plants. Mark turns as soon as we are in. "Hey. I know that guy!" He goes to a man who is setting up a display of his prints. They talk. I shift the weight of my jacket around.

Mark returns. "My mom's friend."

I look at the guy and felt like kicking him. *She's mine, buddy.* "Let's order."

I'm sipping this weird Colombian Chi concoction. It's not bad, but I probably put in way too many sweeteners. I still don't know the breakdown of Pink/Blue/Yellow packets to the regular white sugar. There's this music playing with a lot of bongos and high-pitched yelling. Mark's rockin' along. As are the other customers who are sitting at these round tables along the panoramic windows. It's mellow. I sip my drink and relax. The door chimes.

The girl from the morning announcements and a friend walk across the room. They're so hot even the waitresses do a double take. I turn to say something to Mark. Something witty because I'm cool like that. But he's crossing the room toward… oh no he's not. Damn, he is. He's talking to the hot chicks. Just blabbing away about something. Oh, hell. They're laughing and he's flailing his arms. *No. No.* Now all three are looking at me. I wave and hit my drink with my elbow. It spills across the table and down onto my crotch. They turn away. I madly mop up.

Mark returns. The girls are ordering. "You know them?"

"Yeah." He smiles. "Lisa's in my art class."

"The other one's the morning announcement girl?"

"Angela. That's her name. I didn't know the two of them were friends." He looks back at them. "Hot, huh?"

The girls sit. Mark smiles. I sip my drink and try not to choke. "Come on. What'd you get for Christmas?"

I wait for the girls to laugh at his line. Lisa adjusts in her seat. "The same crap as always. But I did get this new perfume and the most adorable shoes. Seriously, they almost made me cry..."

Holy crap! This kid's a genius. I listen to the exchange and remain mesmerized by Angela's presence. Mark can have Lisa.

"What about you, Ed?" Angela smiles. That same morning appeal spreads across her face.

"Uh... well... uh..." I shift like I'm sitting on a turtlehead. "We didn't exchange yet. My dad had to work. Then my mom got called in. They've been busy."

"No gifts? And you were alone on Christmas?" She leans toward me. Her lips are pouty and full of compassion. I try not to stare. Really. Just like with Mark's mom. Same results. "That's so sad."

I shrug off the lie. "It's all right. We'll get to it."

Angela tilts her head. Her eyes drop and widen simultaneously.

"Yeah, but he had plenty going on the other night. When we got all that snow." Mark launches right into the story. He tells it pretty well, too. Gets the facts straight. I guess. I listen and imagine that the "Ed" in the story is someone else. I have to or I might melt from the inside out. *What is he doing? Hell, he's airing my dirty laundry in front of the two hottest chicks I've ever seen!*

He acts out my fight with the kid in the wheelchair. I look up and spot a plant holder. I imagine strangling him with it.

The story's over. The laughter subsides. He winks at me. *What? No, no. This wasn't fun. You ass...* Angela touches my hand. "I didn't know you have diabetes?" She gives me that same look from before. "My sister does, too." I'm hooked. I shoot Mark a glance. He nods. *Damn he's good.*

"I didn't know you have a sister."

Angela laughs. Touches me again. This is fantastic. "Yeah. Becky. It's been rough." She tosses her hair. "But you know."

Mark and Lisa stand. He escorts her to another table. He grabs some paper from the guy he knows. Sits Lisa down and starts sketching her. Total player.

"I guess I do." I smile. "But it hasn't been that long. Tell me about your sister."

Angela smiles. "It was tough when we were younger. I didn't know what was up with her. I didn't understand what diabetes does to you. I mean, she was always pissed off or passing out." She pauses. Her eyes widen. "But she's good now. Don't get me wrong. She just got married. You should have seen her trying to find a place for her insulin pump. Do you use one?"

I shake my head. I only have a faint notion of what she's talking about. I'll Google it later.

"That's right. Still new. You will..."

I listen to it all. I don't mind how long she rambles. This is the best conversation of my life. She breathes. Looks down at her watch. "Wow. Hey, we're catching a movie. Total chick flick. We have to run." She stands by her chair. "This was fun."

My heart sinks. "Yeah. It was. I hope we can do it again sometime."

"We will."

The girls leave and Mark and I take up our original seats. "Thanks for that."

Mark smiles. "No problem. I saw an opportunity. Besides, I still owed you." He laughs. "You have to use your diabetes as a hook. Girls love guys who need help."

I'm about to say something about it depending on what kind of help, but a knuckle raps on the window by our table. We turn. Sid and three of his new friends wave us out.

All my happy emotions have dissipated. My legs have the strength of Jell-O. Mark's loose though. He didn't put his coat on. I'm wishing I had done the same. What if one of these asses punches my kit? *Jesus, what's wrong with me?*

"Hey, it's Mr. Tough Guy." Sid walks over.

"In the flesh." Mark walks right up to him. Looks around at the other guys. "Gentleman." He looks at the girls. "And whatever you are."

"You know. That's your problem. You just don't know when to shut up!" Sid's face is red. He's pressed right up against Mark. But Mark's got him by almost a foot in height. He's smiling, too. On the verge of laughing.

"That's funny. Coming from you. Considering how tongue-tied you were the other day."

Sid's eyes flare. My stomach flops. Stacy yells. "Just hit 'em! Come on! I wanna get to the party!" She's chewing gum and standing with her butt jutting out like an iceberg. One of the other guys is looking her over. Sid's back goes straight. The other two guys stifle their laughs.

Then Stacy looks at me and her eyes brighten. She stands up straight and puts her hands out like she's holding a paper. "Uh… fate, that is the question. I have something to say about it." Her voice has dropped an octave. She thrusts her head and sputters. The other two join her and do the same. Ashley wipes away a fake tear. The rest of the crew snickers.

Mark looks at her and then to me. He shoots me a pained glance. Turns back to Stacy. She snorts a laugh. Sid's eyes are downcast. Like an embarrassed child's.

"Hey that's a pretty good performance!" Mark says. "You must have learned something from Mr. P's class. I'm amazed. Maybe there is more than one brain cell in that head of yours."

Stacy gasps. Her face scrunches. She walks over. "You don't talk to me like that! Haven't you learned your lesson?"

Mark laughs and turns toward Sid. "I'm guessing this is where you step in." He inches closer. His voice is low and clipped. "Damn, she's got you whipped."

Sid's head snaps back up. He's on fire again. He leans to the side and throws a wide punch. Mark side-steps it.

The quick, blip/siren sounds. Followed by a flash of blue and red lights. They come as pure relief. I look over for the car. Sure enough, 5–0 is on the scene. Sid's group is already clearing out. The cop gets out of his car.

Sid rights himself. Looks at the cop. Me. Then Mark. "This ain't over." He spins on his heel and pulls Stacy by the sleeve. Her voice trails them.

"What the…? Why didn't you…"

Then it's just Mark, the cop and me. "What's going on…?" He stops. "Hey, you're George."

I look at Mark. He's smiling a big grin now. I look back at the cop.

"Zuzu's petals," he says. I am utterly deflated.

Chapter 15

Canst thou not minister to a mind diseased,
Pluck from the memory a rooted sorrow,
Raze out the written troubles of the brain,
And with some sweet oblivious antidote
Cleanse the stuffed bosom of that perilous stuff
Which weighs upon the heart? (5.3.50-55)

"WHO LOVES YOU?"

I pull the phone from my ear. Look at it as if it's going to give me some answer: *Your friend is very, how you say, affectionate, and has great news regarding your love life. He is, trying to be, how you say, witty. Ah, ah, that is it.* Yes, my phone does have a thick accent and difficulty translating. Whose doesn't? "What are you talking about?"

"What are you doing for New Year's?"

I imagine sitting on the couch. Alone. Surrounded by streamers. "Nothing. Why?"

"You want to go to Angela's?"

My brain skips like a rock over water. "Uh... did you... uh..."

"Yeah. I did. *We* got invited. Angela's parents are going to some swank party. She's loaded, you know, and she's got the house for the evening. She invited us and a bunch of others."

My jaw locks. "You're lying."

"That's what I said when Lisa called and told me." Mark chuckles.

"Sounds like you made quite the impression. Don't worry. You can thank me later." He laughs again. "So are you in or what?"

I know that New Year's is going to be a big damn deal around my house. But not in the hey-let's-celebrate-the-fact-that-we're-still-alive way. More in the how-much-wallowing-can-we-possibly-do way. "I'll be there with bells on." I hang up and breathe.

All I have to do is ask my parents. The air in this house is as thick as concrete. My parents have been doing a little better since Christmas. The scrapbook isn't on the coffee table. It's under a stack of muscle magazines near my dad's bench. The tension is still thick, though, because tomorrow is. Simply that. Because it is, and Dad will have to deal.

I just finished reading Act Five, scenes one through five of *Macbeth*. I'd put money on the fact that I'm the only one doing this. I'm not even going to bother to ask Mark. The soldiers are coming to get Macbeth. He doesn't seem to give a damn. Lady Macbeth is dead. I think from suicide. Macbeth goes off about how life has no meaning. His speech is about as upbeat as my dad. I have to go to this party.

I knock on my mom's door and walk in. She looks up from a magazine. I'm taken aback. She's so busted she looks abused. "Hey mom, what's up?"

She sets down her magazine. "Everything all right. Are you low?"

"No, I'm fine. One-fifty-two after lunch." My mom smiles a frown. I sit on the bed. "I... uh... need to ask you something."

She crosses her arms. "All right."

"Well, I wanted to ask if I could go to a party tomorrow."

My mom sits up. Leans against the headboard. "Whose party?"

I stare at my socks. "This girl Angela. Mark and I got invited."

A murmur bubbles from her throat. "Are you going to drink?"

Now I know, with absolute certainty, that I should not have another drink. But I know myself, too. I can't honestly say I won't. "I don't know."

My mom sighs so long, she sounds like a deflating bouncy-bounce. "Ed... you know that you can't drink... I..."

"I know mom. I do. I just don't want to lie. You know?"

She looks at me for a long while. It makes me really uncomfortable. Like when she broke down in front of me. "Honey, I do know. And you should to go to this party... But, can I ask you something?"

"Sure." I'm like a diver standing on the edge of the platform.

"What happened with Sid? The full story."

Now *I* sigh. "It's complicated... but mostly... it has to do with my diabetes. And a girl." I look at my mom. She nods. I tell her the rest.

"At this point in your life, you've got to start making choices." She puts her hand on mine and then says, "And you have to live with them."

I hesitate for a second. "Like with Uncle Brian?" Her hand slithers back to her chest. Her eyes bulge. Then turn to slits.

"Just like that." My dad's footsteps clomp up the back stairs. We both freeze. His rumbling moves down the hall to the basement. We relax. "That's been the hardest one," she says. "The most painful to deal with." Her voice is far away.

"Because you were the one who told dad Uncle Brian had to come off the life support?"

My mom's head snaps to the side. Her eyes refocus. "How did you know?"

I jut my chin toward the wall. "I hear things."

She nods. "He's never forgiven me for telling him what he needed to hear."

A quick shot of anger passes through me. An absolute-bad-ass rage toward my dad. I want to tear down the stairs and beat him for punishing my mom like this. But the anger is replaced by a creeping sense of how he must have felt. I also know that he's not the only one at fault. My guilt hasn't fully dissipated. It tugs again. "I'm sorry mom."

She looks up. "For what? You haven't done anything?"

I shrug. "Exactly."

She stands. "You can go to your party. I'll even drive you there. On one condition." I stand up as well. "Stay safe, so that your father can be left alone."

≈≈

The party starts at 9:00. It's 8:15 and I'm as jittery as a kid without his Ritalin. My clothes look all right and my hair has stopped trying to send messages to the universe. I test: 172. *All right.* I'm fine as long as I'm under 200. Of course Doc Stevens might not agree. I can picture him playing some twisted game of "This Little Piggy" with me. Just to scare me about losing my toes. He'll probably smile through the amputation as well.

Anyway, I'm ready. I just need to do one last thing. I pull up Google and type, "Define, Auld Lang Syne." The second link leads me to a dictionary web site:

Auld lang syne (ôld' lôld' lôld' l', s+n') n. The times gone past; the good old days. Well, it's not much of a pick-up line, but it does seem appropriate.

Mark hops in the car and we're off. He gives my mom the address. A spark of recognition pops in my head. The street's name is real familiar. I don't know why. We roll along and Mark's chatting up my mom. Making her laugh. I'm quiet because the street's name is nagging at me. Like a zipper when you don't wear underwear. At first, it's no big deal. After a while the zipper's cold touch isn't so welcoming.

My mom turns into the development and I'm instantly jealous. There are mansions everywhere, scattered across this sloping hillside like God made his own little display-window winter wonderland. These homes are all like Sid's. The spark ignites. "What road did you say Angela lived on?"

"Fox Hollow." Mark squints through the window, reading the signs.

My brain finds the connection: *Her Web site.* I recall the line in her information box. Twenty-two Fox Hollow drive is home to the one and only, "Tasty Stacy."

"Twenty-four. There it is," Mark yells. My stomach twists like one of those pepper shaker/crusher jobs.

"God damn." My mom stops the car. "Mind if I join you?" This place is absurd it's so big. It's gargantuan. There's a fountain larger than my bedroom out front. It sits in the middle of a hand-laid, brick driveway that wraps around to the front of the house. The McMansion itself is so full of windows, illuminated by so many lights, that it looks like a diamond in a display case.

"No kidding?" Mark shakes his head. My brain seizes. I look to the right, at #22. It's dark. *Thank God!*

My mom laughs. "Good luck boys." She says this like a kindergarten teacher. We clamber out. "Ed?" she calls as I shut my door. I pop my head back in. "You've got everything, right?" I pat my swollen jacket. She lowers her head. Then looks up at me. "Please be careful." I say I will. I close the door and watch her drive away.

⊷⊶

It's 11:50 and I'm nervous. I'm drinking, but that's not the problem. I've decided to drink beer this time. It's got carbs. I won't go low. I've been testing every hour in the bathroom anyway. But that's how I got my nerves revved up.

I stayed in the bathroom for like ten minutes the first time I went in. Two reasons. One, it's gorgeous. It has one of those tubs that spills over into another tub. There's marble everywhere. The sink's like a work of art, resting on the counter like a salad bowl. It all reminded me of Sid's. Which is oddly the second reason. Coincidence.

I figured that I should test one last time before midnight. Who knows what will happen after? Then I started fiddling with the blinds. One popped off the track. The window looks out to Stacy's patio. It's not dark anymore. There's a party all right. Kids are out back grinding to some god-awful music that is pumping from inside the house. The bass is so loud it vibrates Angela's window. I put the blind back in place and tested: 185. *Here goes nothing.*

I exit the bathroom. There's Angela.

"I had a feeling I might find you here. Everything okay? You need something?"

"No. Fine. Everything's fine."

"Good. Because we're going out on the patio for midnight. I've got champagne and balloons."

"Balloons?"

133

"You make a wish and let them go. Like a shooting star."

Oh, I've got a wish. Let's stay inside, instead. I follow her to the living room.

"Everyone grab a balloon and a glass. Then go on out to the patio," Angela announces and turns. I follow her. Mark joins me.

"Awesome, huh?" I go to tell him about what's outside, but we're pushed along by the crowd.

It's cold. I pull into myself and feel even smaller than usual. I look at the patio. There's only a pair of kids out now. *Maybe they're staying inside?*

"This is sweet!" Mark's bombed. Not even trying to hide it. But it's all right. He's a happy drunk. Not like Angela's friend, Veronica. She's in the corner, swaying. There's a clump of vomit in her hair.

"Lesss get on wid dis ting! My assss is freezing!" Veronica's boyfriend holds her up. Whispers something. She goes to push him away but pitches over.

Angela's got a TV out on the patio and it's turned to Dick Clark and New York City. We've got a minute left. I look around at everyone—must be twenty kids—all smiling, holding these metallic balloons that say, "Happy New Year!" My nerves settle.

"Thirty seconds!" Angela yells. We all scream. Someone starts filling the glasses.

"Fifteen!" Mark's got one arm wrapped around Lisa.

"Ten, nine, eight, seven... Happy New Year!" We all cheer and down our champagne. People start letting go of their balloons. I close my eyes. Not to be queer or overly dramatic. I just want to get this right. I let go of the ribbon and watch my balloon disappear into the sky.

"Auld Lang Syne" starts playing. I cross the patio to Angela. "Thanks for inviting me."

She smiles. "Please. You're welcome." She hovers.

"Hey, you know what the title of this song means?"

She tilts her head. "No. Why?"

I lean in and tell her.

"You're so cute!" She bumps me with her hip. I bend down. Her breath on my neck.

"Isn't this so adorable?"

Angela snaps to attention. A cold shot runs down my spine. I know that voice. Stacy appears, flanked by Sid and the rest. Mark unwraps from Lisa.

Angela leaves my side. "Thanks for that. But you can go back to your own party, now."

"Oh, we have your permission? Thanks." Stacy smirks.

Mark touches Angela's shoulder. "I'll take care of this." He turns to Sid. "You heard what she said. Now, run along." Mark does the backward wave thing. Like he's shooing a fly.

"I thought I saw you here." Sid's voice is deadpan. He steps forward. So does Mark.

"Well, now that you *know* it's me, what are you going to do?"

"I don't know what he's gonna do, but I'm gonna beat your little ass!" Stacy charges and almost slips on the deck.

Mark laughs. "She's such a peach." Sid shoots him a look, but has to hold out his arms to brace his girlfriend.

Stacy braces herself. "What was that? Huh? You got something to say to my face?"

Mark smiles. "Nothing that hasn't already been said behind your back."

She juts her hip and cocks her head. "Whatever. Sid, kick his ass."

Sid turns and thrust his chin at his friends. They crowd around. At least fifteen of them. They stand in a haze of steaming breath and devilish grins. I swallow and look at our crew. Skinny and frightened. I clear my throat.

"If you're messin' with Mark then you've got to deal with me." The entire crew laughs. Stacy snorts and holds Sid's shoulder. Sid looks up and then quickly away.

"You don't want any of this. You diseased little freak." Stacy leans in and almost falls on me. She smells like a garbage can full of my dad's empty bottles.

Everything inside me flames. But I maintain composure. Gramps always says, "Never let 'em know it hurts." I back away. "You're damn right I don't."

She looks me over. It takes a moment until she understands. She purses her lips. "Fine, kick his ass too." She shoves Sid. He doesn't budge. She smacks him upside his head. He winces. I can't take it.

"He's not your slave."

"Excuse me?"

Mark pipes up. "Are you really that stupid, or is this just another performance?"

Stacy stands like a parade-float queen. Reaches back. Then slaps Mark. The fleshy, wet report makes me cringe. Lisa steps forward. Followed by Angela.

"Listen, get outta here before this gets ugly." Lisa thrusts her head while she speaks.

Mark spits on the ground. It turns red with blood. He laughs and wipes his mouth on his sleeve.

"Please!" Stacy exhales the word. "What are *you* gonna do?"

Lisa turns as red as the snow at Mark's feet. "You wanna find out?"

Stacy snorts. Leans in. "Yeah." She turns to Sid. "Now!"

Sid looks from Mark to me. He stares for a second. Seems to be thinking. His eyes bounce. But he turns back to Mark and hits him with an uppercut that splits open the night.

I'm staring at the stars. I wonder where my balloon went. I want another wish. The people around me are crying and bleeding. The snow's red everywhere. These skinny kids couldn't fight. But they tried their best. So did Mark and I.

After Sid's punch, the rest charged. I met two. The last time I fought was in fourth grade. And that was really just a wrestling match in the dirt. But I watch enough TV to know where it hurts. I dove and planted my shoulders into their crotches, knocked them back into the snow. But another kid came along and punched me in the back of the head. Sent me sprawling face first into the cold. That's when the skinny guys must have gotten into the mix. Because after I managed to pull myself up, there were guys fighting all over. Sheer chaos.

I got to my feet, head pounding, a lump growing off the back of it. The girls were throwing down tag-team style with Lisa and Angela. It was like those mud-wrestling events. Where they're all wet and sloppy. But then Stacy jumped on Lisa. Wrenched her head back and spit in her face. The other two jumped up and down like cheerleaders.

Sid and Mark were on the ground like two pit bulls. Just twisting and punching and growling. I waited until Sid was on top. I ran over and kicked and kicked until my foot sank in. Sid screamed and slid off. Mark bounced up. Blood dripped from his nose and lip. He looked at me and went to speak. But his eyes went wide. I turned around and caught a fist square in the nose. It erupted. Sent a plume of blood into the air. I sank to my knees and Mark went after the kid.

I kneeled there, cupping my hands under my nose. Blood poured into them. It's ridiculous, but my first thought was *I should probably test. I'm already bleeding.* Seriously, I'm messed up. Then there was Sid. On his knees. Catching his breath and holding his side. He looked over at me and shook his head.

The horizon tipped and I fell to the cold, wet ground. That's where I am now. Sid slunk away. Followed by his friends. Mark came and sat by me. His face is a damn horror show. Angela's bleeding and screaming and holding the phone. Mark says, "Lie down man. You have to stop that bleeding." His voice sounds like velvet. Just like the sky looks in its black crushed softness. Where I imagine my balloon is floating aimlessly.

Chapter 16

Tomorrow and tomorrow and tomorrow
Creeps in this petty pace from day to day
To the last syllable of recorded time... (5.5.22-24)

I AWAKE TO MY MOM'S FACE BEFORE ME. For a moment I think that I'm home. But her eyes flutter and they are red and swollen. I go to speak and taste the iron of blood. It all flows back. I sit up. The swelling juts out under my eyes.

"You're at the hospital, honey. Your nose is broken. But you're okay," my mom says. I take in the room. Feet protrude from under a blanket in the next bed. "Mark." Her eyes narrow. "What happened?" I go to speak, but Mark pulls back the curtain from around his bed. He's got a pile of sterility paper in his lap. A pencil in his hand. His face is so swollen it's like he's wearing a mask.

"Here, look." Mark thrusts the sketches toward my mom. He winces after he speaks. She looks at me and takes the sketches from him. She holds them before her and examines. I turn to Mark.

"You all right?"

He shrugs. "I've been better." He smiles. "But it was worth it." I look away.

"Is this you, Ed? Who are you kicking?" My mom lowers the drawing. Sure enough, Mark has correctly envisioned him and Sid rolling in the snow, pounding away. But he managed to get me too. I'm at an angle. My foot is deep into Sid's side. I point to the picture. "That's me. That's Mark. And *that's* Sid."

My dad and Mark's mom arrive at the same time. She walks in and bolts to Mark's side. "Oh honey!" I look away because I don't want to taint this mother/son moment with something lurid. My dad walks over to the side of my bed.

Like a slap upside the head, it hits me: It's New Year's Day. The anniversary of my Uncle Brian's death. The day my dad finally gave in and told his parents that they needed to pull the plug. That it was only forestalling the inevitable. Here he is. In the very hospital where all this occurred. The very last place on Earth he wants to be.

His eyes match my mom's. He leans forward and examines my busted face. I anticipate the whiskey aroma. It's not there. No beer stench, either. I feel like a slide under a microscope. Staring up at an unflinching eyeball. My heart is pounding so hard that I barely hear him. "Broken?"

My mother nods. "But it shouldn't need to be reset."

My dad frowns. Looks Mark over. Cocks an eyebrow. "Your mother said this had something to do with Sid. What happened?"

Mark's mom stands at this question. As if she just asked it. I look at the drawings. My mom set them on a chair off to the side. "I want it straight from the horse's mouth," Gramps always says. My heart increases its cadence. I clear my throat.

"Back when I got sick. I don't know. Sid and me..."

My dad sighs and mumbles something. It sounds like, "Jesus Christ." He swipes a hand across his face. Steps closer to my bed. "Just tell me what happened *tonight!* I don't care about the rest." He shakes his head. "Goddamnit."

My faces flushes and I stare at my lap. My heart's still thumping and my eyes start to well. I close them. I take a deep breath. The static is back. Like a scream in the back of my head. It's building like a boiling teakettle. Behind the blackout of my closed eyes come images from the past year: the hospital. My uncle's funeral. My parents avoiding one another. Doc Stevens. Sid... I'm shaking. Insulin. Syringes. Bloody fingers. Mark...

The static boils over and whistles out the top of my head.

"You *should* care!" The scream thunders out of me. The static ceases. My heart still thrums. Yet it's a different beat. My dad goes stone. Cocks his head and sets his eyes on me. His lips part. My mom steps to him. "You *should* care about us, but you *don't*!"

My mom stops now. Equally frozen. Whatever my dad was going to say is lost. I sit up. "You're still thinking about Brian, and about who's to blame. You still believe something should have been done differently."

My dad licks his bottom lip. His eyes retreat.

My heart leaps and I have to swallow. "I'm sorry dad, but it was just his time. You can't blame anyone." I pause. Breathe real deep. "Not even yourself."

My dad shuts his eyes. My mom looks at him. To me. Then moves to his side. She clasps his arm.

I wait a moment and slide down the bed toward him. "It's the same with me. I didn't ask for this. But there's nothing anyone can do to change it. I understand, really. I don't want to remind you of that fact. Of Brian. Like that." His eyes are still closed.

"I'll tell you what happened tonight. I got in a fight with Sid and his new friends." I pause. "He and Mark have history… and I couldn't just stand there and watch."

My dad opens his eyes. His face is shifting. His jaw working. He looks right at me and doesn't look away. "I figured you'd be proud of *that*." My heart does laps inside my chest. In spite of this, I keep looking at my dad. He's still staring at me. My mom is holding his hand. She's crying. My jaw starts to work. I reach out and grab my dad's free hand. I take a breath. My insides churn. I hold his hand. I look him clear in the face. "I've done my best. I'm sorry if I've let you down."

I finish crying. Rub my eyes one last time. It's 6:00 AM. I'm utterly spent. I look around for my kit. "Your kit?" my mom asks. I nod. She crosses the room and grabs it out of a locker. My dad's watching. He's drifted to a corner and is quiet now, looking antsy.

I take the meter and go through the performance: 132. *All right.*

I'm about to ask if I can go to sleep, but my dad cuts in.

"Can he leave?" He's asking my mom, but looking at me.

"He might as well stay. I'll bring him home when my shift is over." She turns to Mark and his mom. "I'll bring Mark home, too, if you'd like."

Mark's mom looks exhausted. I'm not even having any fantasies. "Thanks. But I'll probably just stay." She smiles. My mom turns to my dad.

"But he *can* leave, right? He's healthy enough?"

I perk up.

My mom laughs. "He *can* physically leave. But I don't think he *should.*" They stare each other down. My dad shifts so much it's as if worms are crawling under his skin.

"What's up?" My voice cracks.

My dad stills for a second. Looks at me and Mark. Then back to my mom. He answers my question while looking at her. "I have to do something. Here. Now. And I need Ed to come. Mark too."

We all snap to attention. My dad's jaw is working so hard that the muscle looks like it's about to bust through. I pull the covers off my legs. "Let's go." I stand next to my bed. Mark has already done the same. Electricity simmers in the air. Like my dad's some kind of live wire.

"Whoa! Whoa! Just exactly what are you doing?" My mom extends her hands to stop Mark and me. But we get dressed. My dad watches us, turns to Mark's mom and puts a hand on my mom's shoulder.

"You heard what Ed said." His jaw works again. "He's right. We have to fix this. I need him to help me do that." A tear slides down his cheek. He doesn't wipe it away. "Please."

❧

It's like we're in the middle of a war zone. The streets are dead. No one is out. The edge of the horizon has melted from black to blue. Mark and I are swollen and caked in dried blood. But we're wired. Wide awake. Because when we shut the doors to my dad's truck he asks, "What's the address?"

We both say, "Twenty-two Fox Hollow."

The house is as dark as it was at the beginning of the night. Mark and I are standing behind my dad. He looks around and then just opens the door. The house is big and beautiful like Angela's, but it's a trash heap now. Pizza boxes and food wrappers are strewn across the counters and tables. Empty beer cans litter the floor like confetti. There's a kid passed out on the couch and another on a chair. They both look bruised. My dad turns to me. "Where's Sid?"

I shrug. He looks at the kids passed out. Then up at the ceiling. He turns back to the kids and moves toward the one in the chair. He's like a gorilla.

He shakes the kid. Hard. The kid pushes my dad away and rolls into the crook of the chair's arm. My dad sighs and then puts a hand underneath the seat and lifts. The chair topples and the kid spills out. Cans clatter. The kid on the couch pops up. My dad leans over the kid on the floor. "Where's Sid?" The kid blinks rapidly. My dad grabs the front of his shirt and lifts him off the ground. The kid on the couch speaks.

"Up... up... upstairs. Probably in Stacy's room. End of the hall." The kid then turns to us. He recoils. Sinks into the couch like a cornered animal uninterested in another fight. My dad drops the other kid. His head smacks the tile floor. Mark and I follow my dad up the stairs.

He doesn't knock. Just busts in like the cops. He goes to the bed and pulls back the covers. Sid is lying on his stomach. He's alone and he doesn't stir. I look around the room to confirm that this is, indeed, Stacy's bedroom. Sure enough, there are pictures of her and her friends on the dresser, the desk, the wall. There's a giant, metal, gothic "S" over the bed. *Where is she?*

My dad grabs Sid by the back of his underwear and shirt. Lifts him off the bed. He tosses him to the floor like garbage men do to cans. He bounces. Awakes. Rolls over. "What the..." Just for a second his eyes go wide inside his bruised and swollen face. They settle into a pensive, hooded stare. My dad walks over and squats down. Sid tenses.

"Get dressed. We're going for a ride."

I don't know where the hell we're headed. Sid didn't ask any questions. Just walked out of the house with us. He didn't even speak to the guys downstairs. He got in the truck and squeezed between Mark and me. As my dad instructed. He's been staring straight ahead since.

We turn left and my brain sticks. It tries to get traction. This is familiar territory. The edge of town. Out past the church. Up the hill to… the cemetery. *Oh, God, no!* We park and my dad says, "Get out." Not harsh. Not mean. But also not an option. Wordlessly, we obey. Only he and I know where we're going.

My dad squats down before my uncle's grave and brushes snow off the name chiseled into the stone. Sid looks at me. Then over at Mark. Finally to my dad. He stays quiet. My dad stands and turns.

"My brother died a year ago, today. Ed, you and Sid know this. Mark, you may not." He takes a deep breath. "I just want us all on the same page."

The three of us nod.

"What none of you knows is how much he meant to me. How much having a brother *made* my life." I look down. All I can see is that picture. My dad's footsteps crunch over the snow to us. "Sid, I don't know what's up with you. And I don't want to hear the story." His voice is soft. He pauses. I sneak a look over at Sid. His eyes are bugged. "What I do know is what my brother once said to me.

"One time you were over and playing with Ed. We'd just gotten back from a fishing trip. Brian stood next to his truck and just watched the two of you running around…" My dad's voice starts to waver and he coughs into his hand.

"He turned to me and said, 'Look at them. They're just like we were. Damn if they ain't brothers.' I stood next to him and watched. He was right." My dad takes a moment. Breathes a few times. "My brother knew what he was talking about. It wasn't just something *that* day. He saw something deeper. Something you just can't turn away from." He clears his throat. "But things have changed. Ed's got diabetes. You went after a girl. And now Mark's here as a true friend." This weird surge of pride/sadness/desperation hits me. I have to clench my jaw.

My dad squats down in front of Sid. He puts his finger to his chin.

He looks him squarely in the eyes. "You've got a choice to make. Right here. Right now. You've got two brothers. No doubt about it. Ed knows you better than anyone. And hell, only real brothers fight like you and Mark did." He looks over at Mark and then back at Sid. "Your choice. These two. Or just yourself." My dad lets go of Sid's chin.

He stands and starts to walk back to my uncle's grave, but turns and points to it. He takes a moment before he speaks. He looks at each of us. "I'd do anything. Anything to have him here." He looks to the stone and then back to us. "But that ain't going to happen. So the best I can do is honor him by not letting go." My dad goes to his brother. He squats and cradles his face in his hands. My anger toward him just slides away.

For a while it's so silent that I get that underwater feeling. Then Sid speaks. "Ed, I don't know... I don't know what happened." He's crying. Chin pressed to his chest.

"You don't have to."

Sid just crumples. Falls to the ground like he's been shot. He's crying so hard he's bubbling and snot's coming out his nose. Mark and I sit down next to him. After a while, he speaks.

"I just got scared. I mean, I know it's stupid." Sid wipes his nose on his sleeve. "Stacy started coming around. And she was promising all this. Telling me how to feel. She sure as hell didn't want me hanging around you. Because of your disease." He turns to me. "Sorry." I just nod. It's what he needs.

Sid continues. "It just happened so fast." He turns to Mark. "And then you had to tell her off. And I don't know why. But after everything she'd said, I knew that was my chance to get her."

Mark laughs out loud. "So you broke my nose to impress a chick? It wasn't personal?"

Sid lowers his head. "No, just became a coincidence. You and Ed and all." He exhales a long sigh. "Then, I don't know. It all just snowballed after that. Things are crazy at home. Stacy just seemed to have something better to offer." Sid pauses. Looks back at the ground. "Or so I thought."

I think about this, and then that letter. "How do you feel now?

Am I still *disgusting?*"

His eyebrows dance on his head. "What do you mean?" I paraphrase Stacy's note. His face goes crimson. "How'd you get that?"

"You left it with my books."

"Damn." Sid shifts back and forth. "Ed, I'm not disgusted with you. I'm sick of myself. The stuff I've been doing." His voice wavers. Like he's about to lose it again. "My parents are done. My dad moved out. Right before Christmas." He pauses. "Know why?" Neither Mark nor I answer. "Because I came home loaded. They screamed at each other for like a day straight about whose fault it was." Sid wipes his nose. "You know what they *didn't* do?"

I wait for Sid to answer his own question, but Mark does. "Talk to you about it." Sid twists his head fast and looks at Mark. "Same thing with me. Just me and my mom now."

I let them have this moment, and then say, "But you should see his mom!" We all laugh, low because my dad's still in front of the grave. The sun's starting to peek through. It's as if I've been awake for days. I want my bed. But my brain sparks. "So where was Stacy?"

Sid looks straight ahead. "You mean this morning?" I nod. He frowns. Lets out a frustrated growl. "She was with Pedro. I don't know if you know him. I don't even know how he knew where she lives."

I lean back. "I didn't see him... uh... during the fight."

There's a tense moment but Sid shakes it off. "He came after. Since I was all pissed off. Totally not in the mood for her. She hung out with him." Sid clears his throat. "I ended up passing out downstairs, but woke up and figured I'd go find her." He rubs a hand across his face.

We wait for Sid to finish. He doesn't. "And?" Mark says.

Sid sighs. "What... I have to say it?"

Mark touches his nose. "Let's just call it payback."

I laugh. "Yeah, we're even after this."

Sid shakes his head. "Let's just say I found her in her parents' room. She had company."

Mark whistles. "That's rough. What'd she do then?"

"Smiled. She smiled at me like it was some big joke."

Mark's stifling a laugh, and it's killing him.

"I just closed the door and went to her room." Sid shrugs. "I don't know why. Maybe I thought it was all a dream or something."

My dad stands. Wipes his face. Crosses to us.

"Can I have a moment?" He nods and walks with Sid and Mark back to the truck.

I walk over to my uncle's grave. I don't squat down like my dad. I just reach out and touch the cold stone. "Thanks, Uncle Brian." I know that somehow he was listening when I let go of that balloon.

I walk over to the truck. The three of them are screwing around. My dad's inspecting the bruise on Sid's side. "Probably a couple of cracked ribs." He slaps the injury and Sid yells. But it's not angry. Just playful. Mark shields his face.

"Don't slap mine!"

"No, yours is bad enough." My dad laughs. Then sees me. He takes a step toward me and levels his eyes. They're not threatening. "You all set?"

I nod. "You?"

He looks at me with that hard, steady gaze. And for the first time in a long while, there's a certain clarity in his eyes. He looks up at the sky. Now a clearing blue haze. He breathes deep and when he looks back at me he's smiling. "I am. Thanks."

৵৵৹

The customers stare at us when we walk in into Denny's. But it's Denny's—they've seen a hell of a lot worse. I have to test and shoot and do all the other nonsense. I head toward the bathroom. My dad turns. "Where you going?"

I pull out my kit. "I have to go take care of business."

"Bring it to the table."

I shrug. Follow my dad. We settle into a table.

"Y'all ready to order?" The waitress snaps her gum. I'm snagged on a line. I haven't tested yet. I can't order. I don't know if I'm high. Low. Or in between.

"We need another minute, okay?" My dad looks at me.

"All right, just give a holler when you're ready." The waitress moves off to another table.

I take out all my stuff and go through the process: 115. No one cringes when I inject the Lantus. They nod when I say, "I have to shoot, again, after breakfast." They don't seem to care that I leave the insulin and syringe lying on the table. My dad raises his hand and calls the waitress back over. I pretend to yawn so that I can discreetly wipe away the brimming tears.

⁂

I'm in bed. But I'm not asleep. However, I'm not being kept awake because I have to piss. I just finished *Macbeth*. Because I'm probably going to sleep straight through tomorrow. I wanted to finish the assignment. Macbeth dies at the end. In spite of the options, it's what he chose. Maybe that's the whole point. Maybe it all boils down to the choices you're given and the decisions you make. I mean, maybe it was fate that shredded my family. Pulled Sid and me apart. Brought Mark into the picture. Because of fate we all had to deal. We had to figure out what we truly needed and then decide what to do with that.

A low murmur of conversation is coming from my parents' bedroom. There's even laughter tossed in. Not harsh whispers. They struggled through. Made a decision. In spite of the pain, are moving on.

I stare at my wall. The fishing gear. The "what could have been." Something Gramps says comes to mind: "As far as I know this is the only life we get. So no one can tell anyone else what it's all about. You have to do that for yourself." Sounds right. Maybe I'll take Pilsner's advice and write all this down. No, I *will* write this nonsense down. Because sometimes fair is foul. Other times foul is fair. That's just life. That's something normal. It's taken me a while to get this. But it's true. I'm not normal. Who the hell is? I'm something this side of normal. That's a fate I can live with.

Author's Note

I was diagnosed with type one diabetes at age twelve. I remember every detail: my mother's face, the solemnity of the hospital, the absolute confusion. Those images will never leave me and have worked their way into *This Side of Normal*. This book is not my story. It is Ed's. The details of such, however, were hard-won.

Life with type one diabetes is not easy. Every day is different from the last. That is the essence of a chronic illness. Life becomes a paradox: success one day, and then failure the next, without having altered the treatment. It is a humbling experience.

It took me seven years to get this story right. Seven years to gain the necessary perspective. Every moment was worth it. I have been afforded the opportunity to give voice to the millions afflicted with this disease. It is with gratitude that I do so.

I believe I have captured what it is like to be an adolescent today, searching for identity while struggling not to be overpowered by one's own body. It is a unique dynamic, but one that reflects a more universal dilemma: accepting one's vulnerability and entrusting others with our weaknesses. Adults and adolescents—with or without diabetes—can relate. We have all been Ed at one time or another.